"You bought this bathing suit to be spiteful."

"So what if I did?"

Those green eyes seemed to be even brighter out in the sun. They seemed to hold him captivated in a way he'd never noticed before.

"You didn't like the other one," she went on. "You told me to get something different."

"I told you to get a one-piece."

"You don't get to give the orders here," she told him, pointing a finger into his chest. "If you don't like what I'm wearing, then stop looking at me."

Something in him snapped. Luke grabbed her finger and pulled her hand aside so he could step right up and into her face. He held on to her hand as his mouth came within a breath of hers.

"You think you're in charge?" he growled. "You think I can just stop looking at you? Wrong on both counts."

* * *

Tempted by the Boss by Jules Bennett is part of the Texas Cattleman's Club: Rags to Riches series.

Dear Reader,

I hope you are enjoying the Texas Cattleman's Club series so far! I'm thrilled to bring you Luke and Kelly's story. Who doesn't love a good office romance? I love this spin on a typical office setting because this couple is taking their heated fling to the island of Oahu!

Kelly has wanted Luke for years and she's done waiting. Now is her chance as they share a beach bungalow for five days. How can Luke resist? There's only so much a man can take! He's been trying to save his family's company for months and he needs to decompress... Having Kelly to keep his mind off work is just what he needs to relax.

Romantic dinners, couple's massages, sunset walks— the perfect recipe for seduction. Finally, Luke sees Kelly as so much more than his assistant.

I can't wait for you all to take this journey and uncover more secrets with the Wingates! So make sure to clear your schedule, grab your favorite reading spot and your drink of choice because Luke and Kelly are about to take you on a fun ride!

Happy reading,

Jules

JULES BENNETT

———

TEMPTED BY THE BOSS

HARLEQUIN
DESIRE

Special thanks and acknowledgment are
given to Jules Bennett for her contribution to
the Texas Cattleman's Club: Rags to Riches
miniseries.

HARLEQUIN®
DESIRE™

Recycling programs
for this product may
not exist in your area.

ISBN-13: 978-1-335-20950-4

Tempted by the Boss

Copyright © 2020 by Harlequin Books S.A.

For questions and comments about the quality of this book,
please contact us at CustomerService@Harlequin.com.

Harlequin Enterprises ULC
22 Adelaide St. West, 40th Floor
Toronto, Ontario M5H 4E3, Canada
www.Harlequin.com

Printed in U.S.A.

USA TODAY bestselling author **Jules Bennett** has published over sixty books and never tires of writing happy endings. Writing strong heroines and alpha heroes is Jules's favorite way to spend her workdays. Jules hosts weekly contests on her Facebook fan page and loves chatting with readers on Twitter, Facebook and via email through her website. Stay up-to-date by signing up for her newsletter at julesbennett.com.

Books by Jules Bennett

Harlequin Desire

The Rancher's Heirs

Twin Secrets
Claimed by the Rancher
Taming the Texan
A Texan for Christmas

Lockwood Lightning

An Unexpected Scandal
Scandalous Reunion
Scandalous Engagement

Texas Cattleman's Club: Rags to Riches

Tempted by the Boss

Visit her Author Profile page at Harlequin.com,
or julesbennett.com, for more titles.

You can also find Jules Bennett on Facebook,
along with other Harlequin Desire authors,
at Facebook.com/harlequindesireauthors!

I'm dedicating this book to all the women who decide to take a chance and go after what they want. Good for you!

One

"Not a damn thing seems to be working."

Kelly Prentiss stood opposite her boss's desk and listened to him rant once again. Same issues, different day, and burnout was threatening to become a real thing.

Trying to breathe new life into a multi-billion-dollar business after it had hit rock bottom was quite a task for anyone to take on. But Luke Holloway wasn't just anyone. He was the Vice President of New Product Development for Wingate Enterprises, he was her boss, and he'd starred in every single fantasy she'd had for the last several years.

The poor guy didn't even know how many hats he wore.

Thankfully it was Friday, but she knew Luke wouldn't be taking the weekend off...which meant she wouldn't be taking the weekend off, either.

"We need to think outside the box," she offered.

Those dark, brooding eyes landed on her and every nerve ending stood at attention. She thought after working for Luke for so long this sexual tension would cease at some point, but each day that passed she only felt that magnetic pull more and more.

How ridiculous was it to be infatuated with her boss? Could she be any more cliché? Added to that, the man was practically married to his job. He didn't make time to date anymore and, to her knowledge, he didn't even find her attractive. Never once had he flirted or even tried that fun banter men and women engaged in. All work, all the time; that was Luke.

He'd had a failed engagement three years ago and, since the downward spiral of Wingate, he'd poured every waking minute into finding the next big product, or miracle, to pull the company out of the ashes.

Luke either needed some grand new hotels, some phenomenal up-and-coming businesses...or, at this point, some fairy godmother to come save the day. Anything that would give the Wingates the boost they desperately needed to restore their reputation and breathe new life into the family-owned empire.

"You think I haven't been thinking outside the box?" he asked.

Kelly knew he'd been doing everything in his power to rescue the company, but she had to do something to get his attention. Desperate times called for desperate measures and all that. So she had a plan…an extremely *risky* plan. However, if Luke knew what she had in store for him, he'd fire her and never speak to her again.

And, if he realized this scheme was his brother's idea, it might bring an abrupt end to their cozy family gatherings.

Good thing then that Luke didn't know anything about the detailed plans that had been building up behind the scenes between Kelly and Zeke Holloway.

"Listen," she began. "I've been doing some research on my own, and there's an investor that would like to meet with you. He has some great ideas and he's offering to help back the next project."

His brows rose as he listened, and Kelly knew she had him.

"He's ready to meet anytime you're available," she went on, not wanting to give him a chance to speak. "I can clear your schedule and contact your pilot. We could go as soon as tomorrow if that works for you."

Her heart beat so fast in her chest she could barely think straight. Kelly couldn't believe she was deceiving him. But the man didn't look out for himself, so *somebody* had to, right? And, considering she was the closest nonfamily person in his life, she took the liberty upon herself.

Actually, his brother Ezekiel was the one who proudly concocted this plan, but Luke's brother was the VP and had his own host of issues to deal with. Added to that, he had recently married the love of his life, Reagan.

Kelly was the one with Luke day in, day out. They spent hours upon hours together, and she knew how his mind worked, so she prayed she could pull this off. Zeke had told her point blank she was the only woman for the job.

Lying to Luke about an investor didn't feel right. But she promised Zeke she'd whisk his brother away so he could relax and recharge, and considering he was putting up an insane amount of money for this plan, she couldn't back out now.

Silence filled his office and did nothing to calm her nerves. Kelly came to her feet and offered a wide smile, hoping she could at least fake some confidence.

"I think this is the exact thing you need to find your footing," she told him. "It wouldn't hurt to hear what this man has to say."

At least that first part of her statement was the

honest truth. He needed a reset and, quite honestly, so did she. They'd both been working nonstop. She couldn't keep watching her boss beat himself up and she was running out of steam. At some point, someone had to take over and call the loss.

Taking a break didn't mean admitting defeat. It just meant their minds simply needed to be cleared of all the extraneous stuff that wasn't working and to allow for ideas of things that *would* work.

But, she had to be honest here, this trip was also about seeing if there was a spark. She never would have taken a chance on her own, but now that Zeke insisted on getting Luke out of the office and someplace relaxing, this was her only opportunity to take the biggest risk of her life.

"You trust me?" she added, knowing he did but needing to reel him in further to pull off her plan.

"With every secret I have," he told her.

The guilt hit her, but she had to shove it aside. Zeke had every good intention of making his brother take a forced vacation…but her carnal thoughts that were accompanying them weren't so innocent. Still, she had to hold firm if she ever wanted to discover if this sexual attraction was only one-sided.

Kelly figured one minor lie in the grand scheme of things was nothing compared to what Luke had already been through. He would forgive her—she hoped. If this plan procured some new idea, then he might even give her a raise.

Her breath caught in her throat.

And if the plan produced a successful seduction? Well, she honestly didn't know what that would mean once they returned to the office, but she couldn't think about that right now. There was too much on her mind to crowd any more worries in there.

"Ready for me to set this up?"

Luke blew out a sigh and held out his hands. "At this point, I say we give it a try. What do you need me to do?"

"Nothing." Kelly started toward the door. "Just leave it all to me. What time should I have the private jet ready for tomorrow?"

"Let's do noon," he told her. "I can't miss the nine o'clock meeting with my brother. Ava wants to see us."

"Perfect," she said, her nerves now in full force. "I'll make all the arrangements."

Ava was their aunt who had lost her husband, Trent, to a stroke. It hadn't taken much time for Keith Cooper to swoop in on her during a moment of weakness. While he might have been infatuated with her, Ava hadn't returned his feelings. She'd only moved in with him platonically when her estate had been foreclosed. That had turned out to be a mess since, shortly after she moved into her own place, Keith's nephew had revealed it was Keith who had embezzled money from Wingate Enterprises.

Among his many crimes against the family, Keith had used Ava to get closer to the Wingate money and pilfer funds, falsify records, arrange a fire, and frame them for drug trafficking over a period of time. And that's how the free fall had started and how Keith had wound up arrested and why Luke and Zeke ended up hating Keith for taking advantage of their aunt and nearly destroying the entire family.

Really, the whole sordid nightmare was a complete disaster. Kelly was glad to escape from all of that drama for a while, too.

She left the office and closed the door at her back. Leaning against it, she shut her eyes and pulled in a deep breath. She honestly hadn't been sure if he was going to say yes or not, but now that he had, there was no turning back.

So how was Luke going to react when he realized she'd double-crossed him and there was no investor? Not only that, but how would he respond when she finally made a move to seduce him?

The woman deserved a raise, or one hell of a hefty bonus for Christmas.

Kelly Prentiss had stood by his side through thick and thin. She'd been right there through his broken engagement, offering advice and never judging. There was something so comforting about having someone who would not only listen to him no matter what, but who he could also trust implicitly.

Then, with all of the destruction that had befallen the Wingates, she hadn't wavered one single time. She'd put in just as many hours as he had and she had also delivered her sound advice where needed. She was literally his right-hand woman, and he would be lost without her.

Luke had never met anyone more loyal, more hardworking or more dependable than Kelly.

And now she had a lead on a possible investment that could help not only Wingate Enterprises come back from the dead, but could also boost his reputation and get them on the fast track to regaining their billions.

Kelly was still keeping the meeting location a secret, but he counted on her to bring him only the prospects that would help the company. She understood time was of the essence and not to be wasted. Bottom line? If she was so excited about this potential investor and she wanted to keep everything under wraps, then he'd go along with her plan.

His work as of late had only taken him to the office and once to Dallas for the day. Getting out of Royal, Texas was going to be refreshing, and he almost didn't care where Kelly was taking him.

Luke relaxed against the soft leather sofa in his plane and glanced through his emails. He answered a few, but moved the others into their appropriate files to get to later. He'd barely slept last night… story of his life over these past few months.

The stress of carrying a company into a new territory and practically starting over was quite the load to bear. But Luke knew he could do it—he refused to admit defeat or ever give up and Kelly was just as much of a fighter.

He glanced across the aisle to where she sat with her laptop. Her tortoiseshell glasses outlined those remarkable green eyes, and her wavy hair had been pulled up on top of her head. With her legs crossed and her little pink toenails showing through her sandals, she looked like a mix of summer vacation and complete professional. He shouldn't find both attractive, but he couldn't deny Kelly was a beautiful woman.

No, *beautiful* seemed too tame a word to describe all of her complexities. *Striking* and *captivating* were much better descriptors.

An odd stirring shifted through him, and he chalked it up to lack of sleep and an overworked mind.

No funny business could ever happen between Kelly and him. Because no way in hell would he risk his one and only trusted right-hand woman just for a fling. And besides, he was in no position right now to even *think* of being with a woman. He couldn't even get his work under control, let alone have the time to feed into anything such as a relationship.

A relationship? That was so absurd. Clearly he was so stressed from lack of sleep, he was now delusional. Luke wasn't going to be that creeper boss. He respected the hell out of Kelly. Beauty was only part of what made her so special. She was extremely intelligent, with a sharp mind and quick wit. There was nobody else he'd ever want in the boardroom with him, fighting for his ideas and vision…just as soon as he had said ideas and visions.

Damn it, no wonder he was so confused about his unwanted attraction for his assistant. He'd never thought of her in a romantic manner, but now he couldn't help himself. Maybe it was the way she'd gotten a little demanding and a little controlling, taking over this whole plan…whatever the plan might be.

"Are you alright?"

Kelly's question caught him off guard, and he wondered how long he'd been staring at her. The last thing he needed was for her to think he wasn't stable or that he found this look of hers more than attractive.

Damn it, Luke. Get a grip. She's your employee and this isn't a pleasure trip. This is work and that's all there's time for.

"Fine," he quickly answered, then stifled a yawn. "Just anxious to get there."

He hadn't asked for many details, mainly because Kelly knew the ins and outs of Wingate Enterprises as much as he did. There was nothing about this situation he didn't trust her with.

"Tell me more about the investor," he said as he tipped his neck from side to side, trying to stay awake.

Her eyes widened a fraction before she glanced back down at her laptop. "Oh, let's wait to discuss work until we get there. I need to answer these emails. Sutton is looking for the projected numbers as we get ready to finish out the quarter, and it seems like you're tired."

Luke wasn't often dismissed by her, but they'd both been working so hard, he wasn't going to interrupt her now. Sutton Wingate was the company CFO, and Kelly might be Luke's assistant, but she did many things for many people within the family business, including Sutton's twin, Sebastian.

Kelly was an extremely busy woman and she'd put all of this together for him. Luke couldn't help but feel hopeful based on her excitement over this trip.

Finding the next big investment or backer would be the break they so desperately needed once they came up with a plan to revamp their company. Naturally, there would have to be many steps taken. It wasn't just one miracle they were seeking, there were multiple, but they had to start somewhere to get that first leg up on rebuilding.

Luke settled back in and tried to refocus into work-mode. There was no reason he couldn't continue following his own leads on potential investors.

He'd really love to acquire some other jets or bring something brand new to the market that Wingate could sink their teeth into and call their own. Getting in on the ground floor was always the best because, while there may be risk, the only way to go was up and, at this point, they had nothing else to lose.

Unfortunately, his eyes were burning from lack of sleep and he couldn't stop yawning. Any brilliant thoughts weren't going to come to him during this state of exhaustion.

"Why don't you lie down?" Kelly suggested. She removed her glasses and stared across the aisle. "I can move from the couch and take the captain chair. We still have a few hours before we land."

Luke shifted his laptop aside and came to his feet. "No need for you to move. I'll just stretch out right here."

He took a seat next to her and adjusted so his feet were propped up a little.

"I never knew this couch did that," she said with a laugh.

"That's because we're always working, but each seat has its own recliner." He settled in deeper and laced his hands over his abdomen. "I won't fall asleep. I rarely do these days."

"Don't worry if you do," she assured him, staring down at her screen. "I'll wake you when we're close."

He shut his eyes, focusing on the way Kelly pecked away at her keyboard and the hum of the engines. She said they had a few hours left, but he still couldn't guess where they were headed. Maybe the mountains for some resort idea or perhaps the coast to get some inspiration from a cozy town. Wherever they were headed, Kelly must truly believe this could help break ground on a new beginning...

"Luke."

He jerked awake, blinking against the brightness, and realized he had indeed fallen asleep.

Turning his attention toward Kelly, he adjusted his seat to sit straight up. "How long was I out?"

She shrugged as she put her laptop in the case. "About two hours."

Damn, that was a good nap and now he at least felt refreshed and revived.

Wait. Two hours? Where had they flown to? He'd been awake a while before he'd actually fallen asleep. Hadn't he?

No matter where they were, Luke couldn't wait to meet this potential investor. Every time he approached a prospect, Luke couldn't help but think this was the one that would save his ass.

Not that he was in jeopardy of losing his position within the company. He was too powerful and too wealthy to be pushed aside. But damn it, people were trusting him to bring the family business back in a major way. Luke didn't intend to fail and he didn't intend to do half the job, either. He would find the best investors and he would make Wingate Enterprises even more lucrative than ever.

Luke fastened his seat belt as the plane started the descent. "You must be like a security blanket or something, because I haven't slept more than two hours in a row for a while."

Kelly turned to face him with that stern look she always gave just before she lectured him. He'd gotten used to that look. It actually used to terrify him, but he knew his assistant only meant well. She watched out for everyone around her.

Which made him wonder who ever watched out for her?

"You can't save the company if you can't take care of yourself," she scolded. "Which brings me to the reason for this trip."

"What do you mean?" he asked.

Kelly bit down on her bottom lip for just a moment as she held his stare. Something was off. There was a niggle in his gut that seemed to be shooting off red flags, but he didn't know what he should be warned about.

"Kelly?"

"This is for your own good," she told him.

Dread replaced that niggle. "What have you done? Where are we?"

She tipped her chin and squared her shoulders. "We're in Oahu for five days of rest and relaxation."

"What the hell?"

"And there's no investor," she added. "Just you, me, and a private beach bungalow."

Two

Luke stepped off the plane and was greeted with a lei.

"Aloha, Mr. Holloway. Aloha, Ms. Prentiss. Welcome to Oahu."

Still confused as his anger continued to bubble up, Luke stepped aside as the young Hawaiian man, who was dressed in a crisp white suit, placed a lei on Kelly and then gestured toward the large silver SUV.

"Please, come this way," he offered. "We will get your luggage and take you to your resort so you can get started on your romantic getaway."

"I'm not going to any resort," Luke gritted out before turning to Kelly. "What the hell is going on?"

He overlooked the fact that the man seemed to think he and Kelly were a couple and had come here for some lover's retreat. But his mood soured even further when he noticed another man approaching the plane, presumably for their luggage.

Kelly's eyes darted from him to the driver as she offered a slight, nervous smile.

"Could you excuse us a moment?" she asked. "You can go ahead and gather our things."

Once the men were gone and working on the suitcases, Kelly focused back on Luke.

"You lied to me," he accused.

And that's what pissed him off the most. She'd never lied to him, but this was beyond lying. She'd been purposefully deceitful. How in the hell had she planned all of this without his knowledge? Using his own jet? His own pilot?

They'd flown all the way to Hawaii and he'd been utterly clueless and way too damn trusting. She had to have had help, and this reeked of Ezekiel. There was no way Kelly could've handled all of these details, let alone the financial aspect of this, without some major backer...

Like his meddling, yet well-meaning brother.

"This is for the best," she explained. "I've never lied to you before and I've never done anything like this. Don't you see that's how serious this whole thing is? You desperately need a break."

Luke heard her words, but that didn't calm his

frustration and anger. What had gotten into his loyal, honest assistant? Or maybe he should be asking who?

"Did Ezekiel talk you into this?" he asked.

Kelly's eyes widened as her dark red strands blew across her cheek in the warm breeze. He could tell by her reaction that she didn't want to rat out Zeke, but Luke wasn't stupid.

"He told me to make sure you relaxed and ordered me to not let you steamroll me back to Royal before this vacation time was over," she explained. "So, you and I are both going to take a break and recharge. You've been working yourself to death and Zeke and I are not taking no for an answer. Now get in the car."

Luke blinked. He knew Kelly was a strong, determined woman—that's one of the reasons he valued her as an employee and his right-hand woman. But she'd never directed that attitude toward him. This side of her was new and he wasn't so sure he liked it.

Well, a commanding woman could be sexy in the right circumstances, but not when it was his assistant bossing him around like a toddler at the commands of his own brother. Luke would definitely be giving Zeke an ass-chewing about all of this.

"You can't make me stay."

Kelly took a step forward, coming toe to toe with him. Those green eyes seemed even darker now as she narrowed her gaze.

"You're right, I can't make you," she agreed. "But Zeke asked me to do this. He's gone to all of this trouble and your schedule is cleared for the next week. Please, do this for me. Take care of yourself so you can take care of Wingate."

The conviction in her tone had his anger subsiding somewhat. He still didn't like being tricked or hijacked or whatever the hell this was, but he also knew his brother wouldn't have enlisted the help of his assistant or gone to great lengths to get him away from the office if he wasn't worried.

Still, that attraction that had slapped him in the plane, coupled with sleeping so well next to her, would quite possibly lead to them crossing a line they could never return from.

"Can we get in the car?" she asked, her eyes pleading.

Luke glanced to see the driver had loaded their luggage and was waiting by the back door to allow them in. With a heavy sigh, he headed for the SUV. He assisted Kelly before climbing in after her.

Once the door was closed, he glanced over at her. She stared straight ahead, legs crossed, and those glasses back in place. This was his most valued assistant, but she'd been much more than that. She'd stuck by his side through hell in both his personal and professional life.

Never once in the five years that she'd worked for him had she ever asked a thing from him. She'd been so damn noble and now she was clearly worried about his mental state because of all the stress.

Luke swallowed hard. She obviously believed following his brother's orders was the way to go, but Zeke wasn't aware of this stirring deep within Luke. Zeke wasn't the one turned on by his assistant's demands and her sexy little glasses.

But Kelly turned to face him, imploring him, clearly concerned for his well-being, and he would have to be an absolute jerk to ignore all of these efforts. A few days away from the office wasn't something he ever did, especially during such a critical time. However, his brother might have a point. If Luke could rest and possibly recharge his mind to start fresh, maybe that was the way to go.

Hell, he felt like he'd tried everything else at this point, maybe he should spend a few days in paradise with a gorgeous woman. Not that he could let anything happen between them. Because risking anything with this woman would be a recipe for disaster. She was too invaluable to him and the company.

And, while he did decide to stay, that didn't mean he was happy about being lied to.

"Who else knows you kidnapped me?"

Kelly laughed. "*Kidnapped?* Really, Luke, there's no need to be so dramatic."

"What else would you call it?"

"A much needed getaway."

He didn't know the last time he'd had a vacation, but that didn't mean he wanted one with his smoking hot assistant. Working with her in an office setting was one thing, but being in a romantic bungalow on an island resort was a whole different story.

"This might not be the best idea," he told her. "Us sharing a room."

She stared at him for a moment before turning and shifting to face him fully.

"Listen, we're obviously both adults and we're professionals. Besides, we have a house, it's not like a hotel room with one bed. Unless you're afraid you can't keep your hands off me," she joked with a wink.

Oh, hell. That wink and smirk shouldn't affect him, but he couldn't ignore that unwanted pull of attraction. How could this work? What the hell was his brother thinking?

"I'm just kidding," she told him. "Don't look so scared. But I do have to tell you about one rule Zeke was adamant about, and I have to agree with him."

He raised his brows. "Rule? You mean after all this craziness you two concocted, you only came up with one rule?"

"For now," she replied with a grin. "No electronics."

Luke waited for her to tell him she was teasing. When her smile vanished, he realized she was indeed serious.

"You cannot actually think that's going to fly with me." He laughed, then sobered. "How can I check in with work or my brother?"

The brother he wanted to berate for meddling in his life.

"I assure you, Zeke has everything under control back in the office and there's nothing for you to check in on. That's the whole point of relaxing."

"I won't be without my phone," he insisted.

Kelly tipped her head and smirked. "Oh, there will be no phone, no laptop, nothing. You will unwind, you hear me? We will get massages, food and drinks delivered to our private bungalow... And we will have our own beach and our own personal butler, as well. The point of this is to remove yourself from reality."

He stared, wondering just how far removed from his real life he had to be. "I'll give you the laptop, but not the phone."

Kelly laughed, and he found that anger bubbling up once again. He was not going to be bullied through this entire situation.

"I will be taking all of it, putting it in the safe, and only I will know the code," she informed him. "This will be a complete reboot of your system. Got it? You will relax and you will have a good time. I'm here to make sure of it."

The thought of spending five days in a private beach house with his sexy assistant didn't sound like the smartest move he'd ever made. Not that he would ever make a move on Kelly. He valued her too much and would never disrespect her in such a way.

But, damn, being on the beach also meant he'd be seeing her in a swimsuit. If he thought she looked sexy on the plane with those little glasses and polished toes, how would he handle wet spandex wrapping her luscious body?

"Hell," he muttered. "I brought suits…not the swimming kind. I have nothing for a beach vacation."

She threw him a smile. "No worries. I've taken care of that part."

Something about that saucy grin terrified him and he had no idea what in the world he'd gotten himself into. He should've turned right around and gotten back on that plane. Kelly could have stayed and had all the vacation she wanted, he'd even give her paid time. Hell, he'd double it.

But somehow he'd ended up in the back of an SUV heading toward what some would say was a romantic, tropical getaway with his stunningly beautiful assistant.

Seriously. What could go wrong?

Kelly's heart beat faster as they were escorted to their bungalow. The walk through the opulent gardens and tall palm trees flanking the narrow path seemed even more exotic than she'd imagined.

Before Zeke booked this place online, he had shown it to her to make sure it was okay. Like she was going to turn down a free vacation with the one man she'd wanted for years? Any place would've been perfect, giving her the chance she'd been too afraid to take in Royal.

But now, well, they would be alone and there was nothing stopping her. Kelly had gotten online and called the resort, giving strict instructions for her and Luke to be left alone. She'd also gone ahead and set up times for food deliveries, massages, and two excursions to get Luke to lighten up even more. She'd promised Zeke she would do anything to make his brother decompress, and she wasn't going to let him leave this island until she saw an improvement.

As they got closer, the soft lull of the ocean waves lifted her spirits and calmed her nerves. The bright pink hibiscus trees lined the path of lush greenery. Then their home away from home came into view.

An absolutely adorable thatched roof covered the bungalow. The ocean was just on the other side, and she knew their private beach would have beautiful white sand. She couldn't wait to get inside.

"Would you like to explore on your own or do you need a tour?" their guide asked as he stood outside the door.

"We can take it from here," she told him, reaching in her purse for a tip.

"I will have your bags brought down at once," he said, taking the tip and nodding his thanks. "You just need to type the code and the door will unlock. It automatically locks for your safety. Please don't hesitate to call if you have any needs. Welcome to Malie Villa."

Tranquility Villa. So perfect. That name had pulled her in as soon as Zeke shared it with her and, once she'd seen the online photos, she'd been hooked. Never in her life would she have thought to come to a tropical paradise like this. It wasn't like she had a significant other to travel with…she also hadn't been looking. Luke occupied way too much of her headspace.

Kelly typed in the code and opened the door. "Welcome to your vacation," she said, gesturing for Luke to enter. "I'll even let you choose which room you want."

"Wonderful," he murmured as he stepped inside.

Kelly closed the door once she was in and her breath caught in her throat. The view was even more breathtaking than any photo she could ever see.

The entire back wall was comprised of folding glass doors that had been left open to allow the ocean breeze to filter through. There was a private infinity pool and an outdoor eating area. The open living room seemed cozy with all the white furniture with green accents. There was an eat-in kitchen to the right and bedrooms to the left. The entryway had a small Christmas tree all decorated with pineapples and flamingos.

"I'll admit, this place is gorgeous," Luke stated, turning to face her.

Kelly smiled. "Did you think your brother or I would choose somewhere subpar to make you miserable? You deserved the best."

"I didn't think you'd take me anywhere," he countered.

Kelly shrugged. "Well, now you know we'll do anything for you. Even if that means looking out for you when you don't look out for yourself."

He stared at her a minute and Kelly fully realized just how alone they were. They'd been alone at work, at lunch meetings, even in a plane when going to meet investors. But they had never been alone in such a capacity as this. There was something... very intimate about being in a romantic bungalow on an exotic beach with a man she'd been fantasizing about for years.

Could she actually pull this off?

If he was still peeved about being swept away on a forced holiday, she was going to have a difficult time taking a leap of faith with this man that she wanted as more than a boss. She would be sleeping only feet away from him. So close, yet so damn far...

Kelly could never, ever admit her feelings to Luke in a traditional setting. She valued him not only as her employer, but as a friend, and she wouldn't risk her position at Wingate.

When Zeke came to her with a proposition to get Luke out of the office under the ruse of taking him to see an investor, Kelly knew she couldn't let this golden opportunity pass her by. This was the only time they'd be together outside of the office for non-Wingate business. There would be no better option… and what better place than a romantic, tropical setting?

"Go pick your room," she told him. "I'll wait for the luggage."

He turned and went into one room, then the other. Kelly waited in the entryway, wishing they would hurry with the luggage so she could change and explore that beach. She couldn't wait to dip her toes into the sand and water and start her vacation. Though she was a messed-up bundle of anxiety, she hoped she didn't lose her nerve after mentally preparing herself for weeks.

Luke came back out and sighed. Then he unbuttoned his sleeves and rolled them up onto his thick, muscular forearms.

If his bare arms were making her excited, she would be doomed when it came to seeing him in a bathing suit. She'd only seen Luke in dress clothes, or the occasional jeans and dress shirt, before.

"I'll give you the room with the view of the ocean," he informed her. "I'll take the room with the garden view."

Kelly jerked slightly. "You should take the room with the ocean view. The water is more relaxing and I'm so glad to be here, I'm certainly not complaining about a garden view."

"That one has a Jacuzzi tub," he said. "I wouldn't use anything like that."

She hadn't thought about the bathrooms. But she wasn't going to argue. She'd take whichever room he wanted her to.

There was a knock on the door, and Luke crossed to get the luggage. Once he had everything wheeled inside, along with a few extra items, and they were alone again, Kelly took her bag to her room.

"What's all this?" Luke came to stand in her doorway, holding up shopping bags from the resort.

Kelly sat her suitcase up on the stand in the corner. "That's the clothing I requested for you for the trip."

Luke shook his head and sighed. "Who paid for this? You or Zeke?"

She held up her hand. "Just stop worrying about everything. Zeke is the financial backer here, but I'm coordinating all the needs on this end. Your job for the next five days is just to enjoy the view, the food, the drinks, and not think about a thing."

His eyes held hers and Kelly held her breath, hoping he wouldn't argue. She just wanted to have a carefree, relaxing time with him. Selfishly, she wanted Luke to see her as more than an assistant, but she still had to work her way up to that.

Physical attraction had been present from day one. But there was more to Luke that attracted her. He was loyal, kind, powerful, and devoted to his career and his family. There was no way she could've ignored that extra tug toward him as time had gone on and this might be her only chance to make her move.

Time was not on her side right now. But she couldn't exactly attempt seduction on day one... could she?

"Fine," he told her. "I'm all yours for the next five days."

That's what both thrilled and terrified her.

Three

"What the hell did you ask them to send me?" Luke yelled through the closed bedroom door.

There was no way he was stepping foot out of here, not wearing this embarrassing excuse for a bathing suit.

Why was he being punished? Wasn't this supposed to be a relaxing trip? Nothing about this bag of clothes had him calming down. If Zeke was here, he'd likely be enjoying this misery a little too much.

Luke peeked at Kelly through the crack in the door. She stood on the other side wearing some floral cover-up and her long, red hair pulled up on top of her head. She had a beach towel tucked under one arm and her sunglasses perched in front of her bun. Now that was a beach look. What he had on was... hell, he didn't even know what to call this.

Why did Kelly look like she'd just stepped off a magazine shoot while he looked like he was ready to participate in some indecent bachelor auction? Because his goods were definitely on display.

"Just let me see," she told him, motioning for him to come out. "It can't be that bad. It's just a bathing suit. We're adults."

"Oh, this suit is *very* adult," he growled. "Did you tell them to find the smallest suit for me?"

Kelly's brows drew in. "Is the size too small? I didn't know how big your...how big... Uh, what size you'd need."

Her pink cheeks would be adorable in another capacity, but not when his nether regions were being squeezed to death.

"I don't think it's the size," he gritted through his teeth. "I think even two sizes up would be skimpy."

"Skimpy?" she asked, her eyes wide. "I certainly didn't ask for that. Can't you just put on another set of trunks? I asked for them to send three male bathing suits."

"Oh, they sent three," he countered. "They're all the same, but in different colors. Black, navy, and red."

And that wasn't all they'd sent. He'd opened the bags and gotten a sneak peek on the rest of his wardrobe for the week and he wasn't too keen on that either, but at least it would cover up his manly bits.

"Can I just see?" she asked. "I swear I won't take a picture and post it."

She snickered a little and he glared. "I have to say I'm not trusting you much right now. First you kidnapped me—"

"You really need to adjust your terminology," she corrected. "This is a much needed vacation."

"And then you have the resort deliver sacks full of tourist clothing with a bikini bottom only a woman should wear."

"If I'd told you what to pack, you would have known something was up," she explained. "Listen, you're just going to have to come out wearing that and I swear, I won't laugh."

"You already laughed and I'm not even out yet."

"It's out of my system. Promise."

As if to prove her point, Kelly shrugged, causing the cover-up to dip off one slender shoulder. He tried like hell not to look at the swell of her breast just above the bikini top, but he couldn't help himself.

This was *not* ok. None of it. He shouldn't be looking at his assistant's ample chest…and he sure as hell shouldn't be enjoying the way she looked. How the hell would he react when she took her cover-up off? One thing was for certain, she would definitely know if he liked it if he left these damn skimpy bottoms on.

Muttering under his breath, Luke closed the door

and looked around the room for a towel. He grabbed one from his en suite and wrapped it around his waist before opening the door once more.

"Let's go," he told her, holding the knot at his side with a death grip. "You have to close your eyes as I'm getting in and out of the water."

Her eyes dipped to his chest, then lower, before she brought her focus back up to his eyes. Was that desire he saw looking back at him? No. No way. Kelly had been with him for five years and she'd never once acted like she was attracted to him.

He needed to ignore the fact she had more skin exposed than he was used to and remember they were adults and professionals. This was nothing more than a relaxing vacation that she went to a good deal of trouble to make happen.

"No electronics?" he asked.

She held up her hand. "I promise, I put mine away with yours. I won't post anything about your little boy shorts."

Luke glowered at her. "You're enjoying this way too much."

"Possibly, but it's only the first day," she told him. "You'll learn to enjoy yourself, too. That's my goal."

"I'd rather your goal be to call the gift shop and ask if they have real trunks for a man."

Kelly pursed her lips. "I suppose I can do that."

He waited while she stepped into the living room

and used the house phone to call the gift shop. A moment later, she hung up and turned to face him.

"All done," she told him. "Someone is on their way with more options."

"I'll pay for this pair," he told her.

"Zeke's card is on file. No need."

She shifted her towel to the other hand and headed toward the opening to their own infinity pool.

"Just join me when you can."

Luke waited near the door, but couldn't take his eyes off the view…and he didn't mean the ocean and tall palm trees.

Kelly slowly pulled her cover-up over her curvy body and tossed it onto a lounge chair. She adjusted her sunglasses over her eyes and dipped a toe into the water.

That bikini should be illegal.

The scraps of material and strings were just a simple black, but there was very little coverage. They made his bottoms look large.

Kelly stepped on into the pool and then dove under. She came up at the other end and rested her arms along the ledge as she stared out at the ocean.

Luke jerked when the doorbell rang. Clutching his towel in one hand, he opened the door with the other.

"Here you go, sir."

The worker handed over another resort bag and nodded his goodbye. Luke closed the door and slipped back into his room. The minute he pulled out the new suit, he groaned. He wasn't sure which one was worse, but this one did cover a little bit more.

Reluctantly, he changed and grabbed his towel. By the time he stepped outside, Kelly was lying on a chaise on her belly reading a book.

Those damn cheeky bottoms of hers were seriously taunting him. He should not be lusting after his assistant. He respected the hell out of her and his thoughts were taking a drastic turn from strictly professional to highly inappropriate.

Luke blew out a breath. He would just pretend they were in the office. That's all. Surely he could do that, right?

But in the office he wasn't looking at half her bare ass. He never would've made it through board meetings if that were the case.

"There has to be other trunk options than the two I've seen."

Kelly glanced over her shoulder and busted out laughing. "What? You don't like the big red lips on your…um…your…"

He resisted the urge to cover-up said lip section, but instead propped his hands on his hips. "Do I come across as the type of guy who would wear black spandex shorts with red lips on my junk?"

She rolled over onto her side, the sway of her breasts shifting with the movement, and Luke used a good bit of his willpower to keep his eyes on hers. Damn it, he needed a distraction.

"Do you have sunscreen?" he asked. "You don't want to burn."

"I sprayed myself, but I don't know how well I managed my back." She pointed to the table in the corner. "Grab that bottle and just give me a once-over, please."

Luke sprayed her back, even going on down over her cheeks that were only half covered. He sure as hell didn't want to have to rub aloe on her later if she got too much sun. He'd probably go up in flames if he had to touch her bare skin.

Once he was done—thankfully he didn't have to rub anything in—Luke went to the edge of the water.

"It feels really nice," she told him, turning back to her book. "We can go to the beach if you want. Or you can go alone. I don't want to smother you on your vacation."

For some reason, the moment she said smother, he got an instant image of her splayed over him. He was seriously going to have to create some distance between them or he would end up embarrassing himself.

"I think I'll go take a walk on the beach," he told her. "I need to clear my head. You just enjoy your book."

He headed down to the shore at a record pace and hoped like hell she hadn't noticed his blatant arousal. There was no way in hell he was going to make it to the end of this trip without crossing the line with his assistant.

As if he didn't have enough to worry about with Wingate, now he wanted to strip that pathetic excuse for a bikini off Kelly and take both of their minds off their troubles.

Four

Kelly blew out a sigh when Luke left her alone. When he'd stepped outside, she nearly had a heart attack at how sexy he was. She'd known he was built, but she'd never seen him like *this*.

All that dark, taut skin with those black snug shorts—even the red lips right smack in the center didn't take away from his potent sex appeal. If anything, those shorts were damn hot on him, and she thought they were perfectly fitting for what she wanted to do.

The closer she got to trying to seduce him and make the biggest risk of her life, the more her nerves jumbled all together and her common sense told her not to take this chance.

But she had to. It was now or never. So no matter her fears, she had to push them aside and go after what she wanted.

As much as Kelly wanted to admire Luke even more, it was probably best that he went down to the beach alone right now. She hadn't missed the way his eyes had traveled over her body—the man really should wear some sunglasses to hide the fact he was giving her a visual lick.

She also didn't miss the obvious attraction he had to her. Those skimpy shorts hid nothing. Hmm... maybe getting him into bed wouldn't be as difficult as she thought.

Kelly smiled as she flipped the page in her book. Good to know this new bikini was working like a charm, just like she intended. Men were simply primal creatures...even men married to their jobs. They still had basic needs and still craved bare skin and a little temptation.

A fling wouldn't hurt, would it? They were adults and they could keep this separate from the office. She wasn't looking for a ring on her finger or any promise of commitment. The only relationship Luke wanted was his career...a situation she knew all too well because of her father. She'd seen the struggle her mother had gone through trying to get any attention from her husband. Kelly never wanted a life like that, and she knew she deserved better.

So, a little fun in the sun had to be the theme for this trip.

A bit later, the doorbell rang again. Luke was still not back, so she got up and went to answer.

"Aloha, ma'am." The concierge wheeled a cart of food and drinks inside. "Where shall I set up this dinner for you?"

Kelly glanced around and really wasn't sure. "How about you leave it here and we will take care of it?"

He nodded. "Please let us know if you require any further service this evening."

Kelly thanked him and showed him out. She went to the cart and lifted the domed lids. Surf and turf with grilled asparagus and a cauliflower rice. Wine, beers, and a particular bottle of bourbon that she'd requested.

There was also a white-and-gold card advertising their nightly resort entertainment. She was still tired from the trip and not really in the mood to be around a bunch of people, so she wasn't going to mention that to Luke.

Kelly figured the sun would start to set soon, so she carried the plates out to the patio area and set everything up. She poured herself a glass of wine and got Luke a beer, then put the alcohol in the fridge, save for the bourbon that she left on the counter.

Luke still wasn't back so Kelly went to her bedroom and changed into a pair of shorts and a tank. She took her hair down and brushed it, then put it back up into a top knot. The movement had her shoulders feeling tight, and she glanced in the mirror to see she'd gotten a little pink today. She'd have to be more liberal with the sunscreen tomorrow. Apparently she'd gotten so sidetracked with her Luke fantasies and then her book, she'd lost track of time and hadn't reapplied.

As Kelly stepped out of her room, Luke was coming up the steps by their pool. Water droplets ran over his broad chest and beaded all over his close-cropped hair and beard. He carried a towel and stopped by the pool to dry off. Since he hadn't spotted her yet, she felt a little voyeuristic standing here watching him rub his towel all over his very fine body.

Kelly cleared her throat and headed out to the patio.

"You're just in time," she told him. "I hope you're ready for dinner."

"I'll get changed and be right out."

He walked by her without glancing her way and Kelly ignored that twinge of disappointment. He seemed upset about something, but she had no clue what. He didn't have his cell to check emails or take calls, so what could have bothered him on a secluded beach?

Perhaps he was irritated at his attraction toward

her. Luke wouldn't like that he was losing control over anything, especially his feelings. She'd never known him to mix business and pleasure. Even when he'd been engaged, he'd put his career first.

Kelly didn't want more than this right here. She wanted these few days alone with Luke to prove to him she was more than his assistant. Two adults in a romantic resort indulging in a heated fling that would stay just between them was all she was asking for. With the possibility of him finding her attractive, Kelly had a burst of hope that layered over all those nerves.

Kelly didn't mind one bit helping him take his mind off Wingate and everything they'd left back in Royal. She just hoped Luke was ready for all she had in mind.

By the time Luke came back out, he was still scowling, and she couldn't help but laugh when she saw his outfit.

"I swear, I didn't ask them to send all of these tacky things," she defended. "I just gave them your sizes and said I needed trunks, shorts, and shirts. I asked for a pair of sandals and sunglasses, too."

"Oh, I got everything you asked for. But this was the best outfit out of the eccentric variety."

Kelly couldn't help but laugh at the green-and-white plaid shorts and the white T-shirt that read EYE CANDY in bold, black letters.

"I seriously considered putting a suit on," he

grumbled as he took a seat at the table. "And I mean the kind of suits I brought."

"Aw, now you're just being a grouch. It's Christmas time, and we're on a private beach. Perk up. I'm the only one who can see you, right?"

He met her gaze. "Believe it or not, I do demand respect."

"You think I don't respect you?" she asked, a little hurt he would even think that.

"It's impossible to respect anything I've got in there to wear." He leveled her gaze across the table. "The next time you kidnap someone to an unknown destination, maybe at least tell them what to pack or don't have their wardrobe left to the hands of a resort gift shop."

Kelly reached for her wine. "Oh, well. A minor hiccup. It's my first kidnapping."

He ate in silence for a minute, and she wondered if he was literally angry with her for being here and for the wardrobe. She wanted him to have a good time, and by the end of this trip she wanted him to see her in a manner outside of the office and in a more relaxed environment.

Was that too much to hope for?

"How was the beach?" she asked.

He drew his brows together as if trying to think of his day. "Peaceful," he told her. "Having a private beach is definitely a perk that almost makes up for my atrocious clothes. You'll have to go down there tomorrow. How was the book?"

"I'm almost done with it."

His eyes widened. "In one day?"

"Listen, when I get a break I take full advantage," she replied. "I love to read."

"How many books did you pack?"

"I brought seven." She held up her hands ticking off her fingers. "One for each of the five days and two just in case I finish early on the others."

He eased back in his seat and continued to stare at her. "You're really taking this relaxing period seriously."

"You will, too," she vowed. "I have a few surprises planned during our trip."

His eyes narrowed and his lips thinned. "I don't know that I'll survive anymore surprises from you."

She couldn't help but laugh. "I promise you will love them. I'm just trying to help you recharge, remember? You need a little fun in your life and to take time to forget about the office. Trust me, all of those issues will be there when we get back."

He continued to study her, then his eyes dipped to the scoop in her tank. Her heart clenched as the sexual awareness seemed to bounce between them.

"Your skin is pink." He motioned toward her chest. "You need to be careful and apply more sunscreen."

"I know. It's a little tender. I just got lost in the book and the time got away from me. I'll be fine."

Luke grabbed his small fork for the lobster tail. "I've never read anything so entertaining that it caused me to lose total track of time."

"Well, you will have to read something other than spreadsheets then."

He shook his head and laughed. "You're awfully snarky. I bet you're feeling really sure of yourself now that you've succeeded in getting me here."

She clutched her wineglass to her chest. "I won't deny I feel pretty damn good. I was worried about lying to you, but I knew in the end it would be for your own good."

They finished their meal and then carried their dishes back to the cart. Luke pushed the cart out the door and left it for their private butler to get later.

"I did order your favorite bourbon," she told him as soon as he closed the door. "Would you like a glass?"

"I'm actually pretty tired. I might turn in early."

Another sliver of disappointment slid through her, but what did she expect? To ply him with bourbon and have her way with him? No, that certainly wasn't her style. She wanted him to come to her on his own. But she was also going to show him there was more to both of them than work.

Yes, she wanted him to reset his mind where Wingate was concerned, but she also wanted him to see what had been in front of him for the past five years.

Would he ever see her as more? And if so, would he ever admit to it…or would he be too afraid to take that type of a risk?

Kelly sighed. Well, no matter what might transpire between them, it wasn't going to happen on night one. It might not even happen on night five, but she had to try. She had to see if there was a spark between them and if he felt even an inkling of what she did.

When Luke went to his room, Kelly headed into hers to shower and put on her pajamas. Maybe she'd get started on another book. She figured she wouldn't get much sleep tonight…not with the man of her every fantasy sleeping only feet away.

Tomorrow, she would have to make a move. Time was running out.

Hell. He couldn't sleep. The image of Kelly in that damn bikini hovered in the forefront of his mind.

Maybe he should get that bourbon she'd gotten for him. Perhaps a little nightcap would help. It was nearly midnight and he hadn't heard her for some time. He'd listened to her showering earlier and he'd had to think of anything else other than her naked body so close.

There was no excuse for him lusting after her. He'd always found her attractive…any man with breath in his lungs would find Kelly Prentiss stunning. But he'd never looked at her in a sexual way—and now he couldn't see her as anything else.

Damn her for bringing him here and pulling these emotions out of him. Had that been her plan all along? To seduce him? Because she was doing a hell of a job.

He never mixed business with pleasure. He couldn't even hold an engagement together and keep his career. His job was his number one priority. Family loyalty meant everything to him, and in turn, that meant he had to give his all to Wingate.

Tossing his sheet aside, he swung his legs off the bed and headed for the door. Luke had on his own black boxer briefs which actually covered more than any suit he'd been given. He was at least comfortable, though back at home he slept nude. With a thin wall separating him from Kelly, he thought it best to at least have one more layer of protection.

Luke opened his bedroom door and headed toward the kitchen. The soft glow of light coming from around the corner made him pause. He took another step, then another, only to come up short and have his breath catch in his throat.

Well, damn it all. This is not what he needed in his line of sight.

He wasn't expecting to see Kelly standing there in some skimpy, silky blue romper with half her ass on display as she rubbed some aloe on her bare cheeks.

The way she was twisted around trying to hold up the hem of her practically sheer bottoms and rub lotion with her other hand all while trying to see behind her... which looked damn uncomfortable and near impossible.

An instant image of her in various other positions flooded his mind, and he cursed himself for even allowing that to happen.

Her eyes met his and she jerked her bottoms down as she straightened upright.

"Luke," she exclaimed. "What are you doing up? Did I wake you?"

Did she wake him? Hell yes she did. With the picture burned in his brain of her lying in that bikini, of her sashaying with those curvy hips, of her wet body from the pool...

There was no way he could sleep with all of those images rolling through his mind like some X-rated movie.

He remained still, the picture she'd made rubbing her backside now singed into his mind. "Couldn't sleep. I came to get some of that bourbon you mentioned."

And now he would need a double shot.

Luke motioned toward her. "You get burnt?"

Kelly sighed. "Yes. I put sunscreen on, but then I got so caught up in reading, I forgot to reapply. It's pretty painful on my...well, you saw."

He took a step forward, watching as her eyes widened. The unwanted lust and arousal slammed into him, but seeing a sexy woman in the middle of the night wearing nothing but silk would do that to any man…even if the woman was his assistant.

"Do you need help?" he asked. Why was his voice so husky? And why the hell had he offered his services? He couldn't assist Kelly…at least not in the way his body suddenly clamored to.

"Oh, um, no," she murmured. "I think I got it."

Silence settled heavy between them, and Luke wished he'd just stayed in his room. This trip was playing mind games with him, and he didn't even recognize his own thoughts. Up until now everything in his mind had centered on the company, but these last several hours had all revolved around torrid erotic fantasies involving his most trusted employee.

Was Zeke really trying to play matchmaker now that he'd found the love of his life? Was he wanting Luke out of the office to both take a break and have some fling? What was the goal, really?

Ezekiel had just married Reagan in some whirlwind Vegas wedding. The two were so in love, it was almost nauseating and definitely not something Luke believed would work for everyone.

Love sure as hell wasn't for Luke, and he didn't have time for any office romance, either.

"Do you want me to get you a drink?" she asked in that sweet tone of hers.

Luke jerked from his thoughts and shook his head.

"I can get it. I'll probably go sit on the patio for a bit for some fresh air."

Kelly nodded. "Ok. Well, good night."

She stared another minute, her eyes landing on his bare chest, before she passed by him to go back to her room. It wasn't until that door closed with a soft click that he released the breath he'd been holding.

Damn it. He was going to have to pull himself together or he'd never make it out of this trip without surrendering to temptation.

Five

Kelly scooped up a seashell and rinsed it off as the tide rolled in. She ran her thumb over the smooth edges and slid it into the side pocket of her beach bag. As a child, she'd always loved looking for seashells when she'd gone on beach vacations with her parents.

That was something she and Luke had in common; they had both lost their parents when they'd been in college. Her parents had died within a couple years of each other, but Luke had lost his at the same time in a car accident.

Even though Luke was an adult, he and his brother, Ezekiel, were raised by their aunt and uncle,

Trent and Ava Wingate. That's how Luke and Ezekiel had slid into the company.

Unfortunately, Trent passed away and a griev-
ing Ava had turned to Keith Cooper...who ended up
being the downfall of Wingate, but that bombshell
fact didn't come out until a very carefully placed
wiretap.

The downward spiral of the company just seemed
to steamroll with one unfortunate event after another
between fake charges being brought against them,
foreclosures of properties, and the embezzlement.
Keith had been behind it all and would certainly
pay for his crimes.

Sutton Wingate, the CFO, was doing all he could
on his end to make the numbers work, but there just
wasn't a way to bring this company back up from the
ashes without some grand new project to give them
that boost they needed.

That's why Ezekiel and Luke were feeling the
pressure to make things right and eliminate the black
cloud that had been looming over Wingate Enterprises.

The stress had just become too much and while
Zeke had Reagan as an outlet, Luke only had his
career. That's when Zeke had realized his brother
needed to get away and clear his head.

Between all of the career ups and downs, Luke
had been put through the ringer, but so had his personal life with the broken engagement a few years

ago. Kelly had never been as happy as when his ex, Lily, had finally gotten out of his life. And as far as she was concerned, Lily had never been good enough for Luke. She'd been much too demanding, not understanding that Luke had an important role in Wingate and couldn't just take off on a whim. She never cared about Luke's feelings or his work, she had only cared about how big her ring was, or how fancy their wedding could be or having the grandest house in all of Royal, Texas.

And Kelly couldn't stand how Lily would look down on her when she came into the office. Like being an assistant was so far beneath a wanna-be trophy wife.

So when all was said and done, the broken engagement was for the best. Luke wasn't the marrying kind and clearly Lily didn't see that. Kelly knew exactly the type of man he was…and that's the sole reason a fling was her only option with the man she was so hopelessly infatuated with.

Moving on down the beach, she slid her toes along the wet sand where the tide kept coming in. She felt another larger shell and bent down to dig it out and rinse it off, too. Although she didn't know how long she'd walked, so far she'd found five shells that she wanted to take back to Texas. She wanted a reminder of her trip to this beautiful, exotic location.

And her trip with Luke.

That sounded ridiculous and naive, but she was the boss of her own little world and she didn't care.

She didn't see Luke this morning when she'd gotten up. Breakfast had been delivered at nine. She'd grabbed some fresh fruit and drank a mimosa before leaving and still hadn't heard a peep from his bedroom.

Maybe he was hiding or embarrassed after last night. Perhaps he was trying to figure out how to face her since he'd seen her bare ass?

All she knew was she hadn't missed the way he'd looked at her. The lighting might have been dim, but the raw passion in his eyes had been damn obvious.

He'd been turned on and those tight, black boxer briefs did nothing to hide the fact he'd also been aroused.

Likely seeing any half-naked woman in the middle of the night would cause him to get turned on, but he'd never been turned on by her before…at least not that she knew.

Kelly turned and headed back toward the bungalow. She put on her yellow bikini and only threw on a white wrap around her waist. While she definitely needed less sun on her buns today, she still wanted to go back and get more sunscreen on her upper body.

She rinsed off her feet at the outside shower and left her bag and sandals on the chaise by the pool. The sun was already beating down and she couldn't wait to build on the tan she'd started.

Being stuck in an office for ten hours a day lately, she hadn't had much time for catching some rays. Not to mention December wasn't the best month to try to gain some color in Texas.

When she stepped into the bungalow, Luke stood at the breakfast cart picking at a piece of bacon. He glanced up and caught her eyes.

"Sleep well?" she asked, not really knowing how to break the ice. She also figured he hadn't slept too well if he'd needed the aid of some hard alcohol to assist him.

What was the protocol after your boss saw you rubbing your bare ass with aloe? Should she make a joke? Offer to rub *his* ass?

No, Kelly. Calm down. He was still her boss, he still deserved respect. She was just going to have to take this one minute at a time to see how he was going to handle everything.

The man had enough chaos in his life and here she was adding to his angst. She didn't want his worries to grow, she wanted to seduce him. She hadn't seduced a man before and she was starting to wonder if she was even able.

"After the bourbon and fresh air I slept fine," he muttered.

Okay. Well, clearly someone wasn't a morning person. He was always ready to go in the office in the mornings. How could he not be at such a dream-like location? This place made her forget her worries...except for the fact she was sexually frustrated.

"I'm sorry about last night." Might as well bring out the proverbial elephant. "I found the aloe in the fridge so I just stood in here and applied it. Had I known you were awake, I never would've..."

He stared. Those dark eyes seemed to bore into her as if trying to uncover her deepest thoughts. He'd put on a pair of green shorts with a floral, very tacky button-up, but he'd left it completely open. How could the man make a tasteless tourist wardrobe look so darn sexy?

Maybe it was that bedroom glare, maybe it was the dark, black beard, maybe it was that exposed chest that made her want to run her hands over the taut muscles and chest hair... Or maybe it was the *entire* package that was still driving her out of her ever loving mind.

She'd asked for this. After all, she was the one who had brought him here under the guise of work. What did she expect? Of course his body would be on display. They were on a tropical island and the weather called for skin to be out...not covered up.

If only she had the green light to touch said skin she wouldn't be so cranky and frustrated.

Kelly cleared her throat. "Anyway, I'll be sure to stay in my room at night," she promised as she moved closer to grab a slice of pineapple. "The beach is beautiful. I found some really nice shells. I always collect some anytime I get to a beach. I keep a bowl of them on my desk at home to calm me when I'm feeling stressed."

He stared at her and she wondered why she'd started babbling and telling him random nonsense.

"Are there plans for the day?" he asked, clearly not impressed by her small talk.

She smiled. "Actually, yes. Later today we are getting a massage."

He stared at her once again. "A massage?"

"It's pretty much key to relaxing, Luke. I promise, you'll love it."

"Don't count on that," he told her. "I'd love to get my phone and check my work emails. That's what I'd love."

Kelly rolled her eyes and grabbed a strawberry. "Not going to happen. So, you want to swim or go to the beach or walk around the resort?"

"I don't even know what to do."

She couldn't help but laugh. "That's why I'm here," she informed him. "I'm going to teach you to relax."

"I'll relax when I think of a solution for Wingate."

Kelly actually felt sorry for him. He was wound so tight he couldn't think of anything else. She seriously had her work cut out for her.

"You know when you'll think of it?" she asked. "When you're not *trying* to think of it. I know that sounds strange, but it's the truth."

He reached for another piece of bacon and bit into it, then turned a mug over and poured coffee from the carafe. She waited while he sipped his java and continued to pick around at the breakfast.

"Why don't you get some trunks on and we can take a walk on the beach," she suggested.

"Didn't you just do that?"

"It's more fun with someone else."

"What do you do for fun back in Royal?" he asked curiously.

She'd worked for him for five years, and he knew most things about her, but she realized he never really asked about her personal likes or hobbies.

"Lately I've been too tired to do much else other than work, grocery shop, and do my laundry," she admitted. "I love to read and travel when I can. I've always been a beach girl at heart. Growing up we always vacationed at the shore. My parents chose a different beach locale each summer, so I guess that's where my love of travel also comes into play."

His brows drew in. "You haven't taken a vacation in the five years you've worked for me."

"No, I haven't," she agreed, pouring herself another mimosa. "When I first started working I wanted to be there to make a good impression and I couldn't afford to travel. Then everything went to hell. I couldn't leave when you needed me most. And now that we're trying to regain our footing and re-build, I couldn't just take off."

"Yet you did," he reminded her.

She leveled his stare. "Because you're working yourself to death, which wasn't helping anyone. You'd gotten cranky with the staff."

"You mean with you," he corrected.

Kelly took a drink and shrugged. "I can handle your growling, but when I see that it's not just a bad day here and there and you're starting to form a long-term pattern, I need to intervene. I care for you, Luke."

There. She'd put that nugget of information out in the open and he could take the statement the way he wanted.

A corner of his mouth kicked up in amusement. "Are you my self-appointed keeper?"

She crossed her arms, still holding onto her mimosa. "I'm your assistant. I wear many hats under that title."

"Did you and my brother have a long talk about me?" he asked.

"We did. He's just as concerned as I am."

Luke sighed and raked a hand over his beard, the bristling against his palm had all of her nerve endings standing on edge. She could practically feel that coarse hair along her bare skin as he pleasured her.

"Then why didn't he say anything?"

Luke's demanding question brought her back from her fantasy. "Did you want Zeke to take you on a getaway?"

His eyes slowly ran over her body, giving her even more ammunition for her arousal. How could the man be so potent when he wasn't even touching her?

"We both can't be away from the company," he stated, his eyes darting back to hers. "Ava is just getting back into the swing of things and we need to support her all we can."

Kelly was proud of the fierce woman Ava Wingate had proven to be. After Keith had been pilfering money over time and destroying everything they had, she had decided to jump back into Wingate and make the company stronger than ever.

She was still fragile from all the heartache, but she'd always been a strong role model for Luke and Zeke.

"Then don't you think you should just listen to me?" Kelly asked. "Ava needs you at the top of your game, and one week will not make or break the company. With her and Zeke there, everything will run just fine. After all your family has gone through, I think you can take this time to regroup."

Luke came around to the other side of the breakfast cart to stand next to her. He continued to stare at her like he could read her thoughts…which was terrifying if he knew what she'd been thinking about him.

"Fine," he stated. "For the next five days, I'm yours. Do what you want."

Kelly nearly stripped his clothes off, but regained

her common sense before embarrassing herself. The next five days would surely prove to be extremely memorable…and maybe just a little thrilling.

Six

"Are we having fun yet?"

Kelly laughed and he hadn't realized how sexy that soft chuckle of hers could be. Maybe it was because he was lying within inches of her on their private patio or perhaps it was due to the fact that his eyes were closed and his other senses were heightened. Or maybe it was because she kept wearing the skimpiest damn bikinis he'd ever seen.

"I'm having a blast," she answered.

"I'm not doing anything but sitting still," he grumbled.

"That's the point."

That made no sense to him. He needed his phone,

he needed to be setting up meetings of potential investors, he needed... Hell, he needed to be doing something. He'd never just sat still before. What did that accomplish?

And not only was he sitting still without his work, he had to be subjected to this unwanted jolt of desire every single time he was around Kelly.

Which was all the damn time.

"Is Ezekiel meeting with—"

"No work talk," she demanded.

Luke sat up and swung his legs over the side of the chaise so he could face Kelly. She continued to lie there with her eyes closed, driving him crazy with those little yellow strings tied at her hip bones, and he knew good and well she heard him sit up. The woman might be the death of him.

If he didn't know better, he'd think she was doing this on purpose.

"How come you aren't this annoying in the office?"

Now she did turn to face him, pulling an arm over her forehead to shield the sun as she flashed him a smile.

"Because you're in charge in the office," she told him. "I'm in charge here. If you're getting restless, we can take a walk around the resort or down on the beach."

"I need to do something other than sit here."

She abruptly came to her feet and motioned for

him to get up, too. "Go throw on something else and we'll take a walk. The resort is beautiful. We can go have a drink or something."

That sounded somewhat better. At least she'd be wearing more clothes, which would certainly help his mental state…and his growing attraction. He absolutely could not see Kelly as more than a friend or assistant. He refused.

Which is why he was going to push away all of those mental pictures of her in those damn bikinis and remember he was her boss. He could not cross that invisible line because there would be no coming back.

Kelly would much rather spend her time relaxing on the beach and catching some rays, but if Luke wanted to walk around, she'd go with him.

They made their way along the paved paths through the lush gardens and past other bungalows. The few couples they saw were walking arm in arm or holding hands. Kelly bit the inside of her cheek to keep from laughing. Probably not many boss/assistants on romantic getaways.

"Do you want to look in the gift shop?" she asked. "Maybe you'll find some other things to wear that aren't so bad."

Luke glanced her way and nodded. "Couldn't hurt."

"I mean, you do look like a tourist, so that's what

you are. But if the plaid, floral, and tacky tees aren't doing it for you, then I guess we can shop."

"You are seriously getting your kicks out of this," he chuckled. "I'm sure you can't wait to get back to tell my brother."

Kelly laughed. "Oh, he'll definitely be informed of how well we spent his dollars."

They passed a couple of restaurants, one Mexican and one Italian. There was a buffet on the other side of the resort and a few other themed restaurants. Kelly loved that they could order from any of the places, or a combination of them, for any meal. So far, everything they'd eaten had been amazing.

They passed workers who merely smiled, nodded, and murmured a polite Aloha. Everything was so laid back and easy going here.

Luke reached the gift shop door and reached to open it, gesturing for Kelly to enter first. Even though he was a tad disgruntled, that Southern charm was always present.

"Aloha," the pretty female worker greeted. "What can I help you find?"

"We're just looking," Kelly told her with a smile.

"Let me know if you need any help."

Luke went immediately to the men's section and began perusing the swim trunks. Nearly everything was small, skimpy, and extremely garish. Kelly picked up a pair of boxers that claimed they glowed in the dark with little lips all over the material.

Kelly held them up and smiled, shaking the hanger. "How about a pair of boxers to match your trunks?"

He glared at her over the rack. "I've got my own, thanks."

She shrugged and hung them back up. "You can look here. I'm going to check out my section."

"See if you can find a suit that covers more," he muttered.

Kelly jerked. "Excuse me?"

His eyes met hers. "A one piece or something."

Irritation quickly slid into anger. "So you want me to get a different suit?"

"That would be nice."

She offered a sweet smile. "Sure thing. Anything to make you relaxed."

Turning toward the bathing suits, Kelly started searching for the perfect one. She found something in white that she believed would work just right. She also selected a cute little backless sundress in a pale pink and a pair of colorful sea glass earrings.

Kelly went to the register and had everything charged to her card because she wasn't putting it on the room for Zeke to pay for. She grabbed her shopping bag and turned to see Luke empty-handed.

"Nothing capture your attention?" she asked.

He shook his head. "I'll make do with what I have."

Kelly shouldered the shopping tote and headed

toward the door. "Well, I have a new suit so what do you say we grab some drinks from the bar and head back to the room? We can get changed and go down to the beach for a few hours."

"I could use a drink," he agreed.

As soon as they stepped outside, they headed to the bar closest to their hut and grabbed a few tropical cocktails. Kelly couldn't stand the silence or the questions nearly exploding in her mind.

"What was your issue with my suit?" she asked as they walked side by side.

"What suit?" he grumbled. "You've been wearing scraps."

Kelly bit the inside of her cheek. She wasn't sure if she should be pissed or amused. Either way, he noticed her and he was irritable. That was a great sign that her plan might be working.

"I'm getting sun and I'm on vacation," she reminded him. "Everyone has a home wardrobe and a vacation wardrobe."

"Not me."

She rolled her eyes as she sipped from her hot pink straw. "I'm not surprised," she retorted. "You don't go anywhere to need a vacation wardrobe."

They reached the door and he punched in their code. Luke held the door open for her and she brushed by him as she entered. She hadn't done it on purpose, but there wasn't much room. A small thrill shot through her. She didn't miss his swift intake of breath or the way that hard, muscular body felt against her own. Granted the moment only took a second, but it was enough to have her wondering if he was finally seeing her in a different way.

"I'll get changed," she told him as she headed toward her room. "Meet you out on the patio in five minutes."

"I've never known a woman who can get ready that fast."

Kelly tossed a glance over her shoulder. "It's the beach, Luke. There's not much to do. Besides, you've never been with a woman like me."

Seven

Luke stepped from his room just as Kelly did. He shouldn't have said a damn word about that bathing suit. Because he couldn't run the risk of her realizing that she was getting to him.

In any event, he hoped like hell she got something that covered her butt cheeks and her boobs. Maybe she found one of those surfer-style suits with the higher neck and sleeves. That would certainly help.

Or maybe it wouldn't. Kelly Prentiss was a hell of a beautiful woman. Even in the office, she was a head-turner. When they'd go out for meetings in restaurants or to meet potential investors, she definitely got the attention of men.

"Ready to go?" she asked, holding onto her straw bag.

At least she had on a cover-up that he couldn't see through. She'd tied the wrap around her waist and pulled her hair up on top of her head. Just a few pieces fell down along her neck, caressing her creamy skin.

He seriously had to think of anything else so he didn't give away exactly what he was thinking. These damn lip bottoms didn't hide a thing.

"Let's go."

"I also have the butler bringing more drinks," she said as she headed toward the patio. "I told him we'd be on the beach so he is bringing them down there along with some snacks."

She thought of everything. If he wasn't so turned on by her, and angry with himself for allowing those unbidden emotions to slip in, he'd be impressed with how she continued to stand by him.

He couldn't deny that he would've been lost these past five years without her. From having his back in board meetings to rallying around him emotionally during the crisis, Kelly was one of the strongest, most loyal women he knew. She was absolutely invaluable to him in all aspects of his life.

He followed her down to the beach and to the cabana they had. Kelly sat her bag down and reached for the tie of her wrap. Luke adjusted his sunglasses and slipped off his flip-flops, turning them over so the sun didn't make them too hot.

When he glanced back up, he nearly choked.

"What are you doing?"

Kelly glanced to him, her hand in her straw bag. "Getting sunscreen," she said as she pulled out the green can.

"What the hell is that suit?" he demanded.

She glanced down, then back up. "You told me to get a new one. You like?"

She did a slow turn. The top barely covered her nipples and the back... Luke swallowed...was a damn thong.

"No, I don't like," he growled. "You're my assistant."

Kelly laughed as she sprayed her arms. "Does my status change with each suit?"

Luke rubbed his jaw. "You can't... I can't—"

She stopped spraying and stared at him.

"This isn't right," he bit out.

"What?"

He motioned with his arms, pointing toward her very tempting display. "All of this. You, me...all of your bare skin. You're my assistant."

Her lips quirked in a grin. "You keep saying that, Luke. I'm well aware of my job title, but right now neither of us are working. I assure you, if I was another woman on vacation with you, this bathing suit wouldn't be a problem."

She went back to spraying herself, totally ignoring him. Luke clenched his jaw. *Nobody* ignored him. And when the hell did she get so mouthy? Was she trying to drive him out of his mind?

Luke moved around the cabana, his eyes locked on her gorgeous body. He stopped inches from her and she instantly stopped spraying to stare up at him.

"Need some spray?" she asked, holding up the bottle.

"I need you to stop this," he commanded. "What are you doing to me?"

"Forced vacation, remember?"

He jerked his sunglasses off and tossed them to the cabana bed before doing the same with hers. He wanted total honestly and he needed to see her eyes to try to get a read on exactly how she was feeling.

"You bought this suit to be spiteful."

"So what if I did?"

Those green eyes seemed to be even brighter out in the sun. They held him captive in a way he'd never noticed before.

"You didn't like the other one," she went on. "You told me to get something different."

"I told you to get a one-piece."

She cocked her head and tipped her chin in a defiant manner. "You don't get to give the orders here," she reminded him, pointing a finger into his chest. "If you don't like what I'm wearing, then stop looking at me."

Something in him snapped. Luke grabbed her finger and pulled her hand aside so he could step right up and into her face. He held onto her hand as his mouth came within a breath of hers.

"You think you're in charge?" he growled. "You think I can just stop looking at you? Wrong on both counts."

Luke leaned in, gazing into her eyes for a moment, silently making sure she was definitely on board. The intense desire staring back at him gave him no reason to stop.

He claimed her lips, ready to put them to better use than sassing him.

Never in his life had he wanted to kiss anyone more. He'd never been more sexually frustrated in such a short time and he'd never in his wildest dreams thought he would want his assistant in such a carnal manner.

Damn this woman could kiss. Her nearly bare body pressed against his as she met his passion with a heated desire all her own. He still held onto one of her hands, but her free hand came up to the back of his neck, as if holding him in place…

Had she been keeping this inner vixen bottled up? Did she have feelings for him or was she just taking advantage because he'd gotten in her face?

He didn't give a damn right now. There was a need, an ache that he needed to feed. Something burning inside of him that he'd suppressed for far too long.

Kelly's hips ground against his, and there was absolutely no denying exactly how aroused he was. No matter how irritated he tried to be, she knew the truth now.

"Excuse me, Miss Prentiss."

They jerked apart, his hand still holding hers as he turned to look over her shoulder. The butler stood there with a large tray full of snacks and drinks.

"I'm sorry to interrupt," he went on. "I just didn't know where you wanted these?"

Kelly stepped back from Luke and eased around him. "Thank you so much," she said sweetly. "Just set everything here."

She pointed to the table next to the cabana and pulled money from her bag for a tip.

Once the butler left them alone, Kelly turned back to face him. Her lips were swollen and damp, and he had to clench his fists at his sides to keep from closing the gap between them and finishing what he'd started.

"Are we going to talk about that or do you just want a drink?" she asked.

Was she seriously just going to move on to the refreshments? Like what just happened hadn't taken them across some invisible line they could never come back from?

"How long have you wanted to kiss me?" he asked bluntly.

"You kissed me first," she retorted. "So I guess I should be asking you that same question."

Fair enough.

"For about a day now."

She crossed her arms and shifted her hips as those breathtaking green eyes continued to hold him in place. "Well, I've been coveting your kiss a little longer. You didn't disappoint."

Kelly didn't say another word as she reached for one of the tall piña coladas with a bright pink flower on the side of the rim. She eased the flower out of her way before taking one long drink.

"This is amazing," she said, going in for another sip. "You ready for one?"

"How long?" he asked again, his patience at an all-time low.

Holding onto her glass, she glanced over her shoulder. "Years."

Luke remained still, absolutely stunned at her admission. How had he not known? How had he missed the signs? She'd never said one word or even flirted.

"That's a long time to keep your emotions to yourself," he told her.

"You were engaged and my boss, so that's not exactly a time to reveal my inner desires."

Desires. That word slipping through her lips had his body aching even more. He'd always known she

was beyond brilliant, independent, strong-willed...
but sexy hadn't entered his mind. And now that's the
only word he could use to describe her.

"You didn't think I deserved to know before
now?" he demanded, taking another step toward her.

"And when would that conversation have taken
place, Luke? During a meeting where we were all
stressed trying to bring the company from the ashes?
Or maybe when your engagement fell apart? Tell me
when exactly I should have opened up my most vulnerable thoughts to you."

When she sounded like that, so exposed and bold,
he felt like a complete jerk.

Luke pulled in a deep breath and propped his
hands on his hips to keep from touching her again.

"Would you have ever said anything?" he asked
softly.

She dropped her arms at her sides. "I was letting
my swimsuits speak for me."

He said nothing. What was there to say? He was
sinking here and there was absolutely no lifeline anywhere in sight.

"Listen," she started. "We kissed. We don't have
to do anything else. My attraction to you doesn't
have to change anything, either. It's not like you're
the only guy I find sexy."

Luke moved before he even thought about his actions. His feet slid through the sand as he shifted to
stand directly in front of her.

"Do you kiss those other guys like that?" he demanded.

She tipped that chin again and he was finding he wanted to nip at that as well. There had been way too damn much brought to his attention in the past day and he still wasn't sure how he felt about that... But he knew he needed to fix this ache, this gnawing need he had.

"I don't believe that's any of your business," she answered pertly.

"You just threw other men in my face," he countered. "You made it my business."

Her lips quirked in a grin and her eyes sparkled with mischief. "So what are you going to do with all of this information?"

Was she challenging him? Luke didn't know if he was amused, turned on, or peeved. Likely a healthy dose of all three.

"Figure out where the hell my mind is at."

He left her standing there as he went straight to the ocean, welcoming the cool water in a vain attempt to calm his raging hormones.

What the hell was he going to do? she'd asked. He had no idea, but he was stuck alone with her for four more days, and he had a feeling that kiss was a stepping stone to something much more.

Eight

As much as Kelly had wanted to follow Luke into the ocean, she'd decided they needed space. She lay on the cabana with her drink, and his since he ran away, and picked up her book.

Since the white material draped all across the top of the cabana, she didn't need sunscreen after all. She lay on her stomach reading, popping the fresh fruit and enjoying their piña coladas.

And thinking about that kiss.

Mercy, her boss could make a woman's toes curl. Her suit nearly melted off and that had nothing to do with the heat. The way he'd grabbed her, com-

manded her without a word, and then claimed her...
Kelly's wildest fantasies hadn't even been that good

What would happen if they did more than kiss? If
her entire body had responded to just his lips, would
she be able to even handle more?

Oh hell yes she could. She'd been dreaming of
that moment for quite some time. As much as she
found Luke attractive and sexy and intelligent—and
pretty much the perfect man in every way—she also
knew a workaholic like him would never share his
life with a woman... Not when he had such a demanding career. Kelly had known that in advance,
which is why she always told herself if she ever got
the chance with him, they could only be physical.
Nothing more.

She flipped the page in her book and took another
sip of her drink. The sand shifted and water droplets
splattered onto her legs.

Glancing over her shoulder, she saw Luke raking
a hand over his hair, clearly the source of the droplets. She thought she'd only give him a glance, but a
body like that really deserved so much more.

All of that dark skin with water clinging to those
impossibly broad shoulders and then losing the fight
as the moisture slid down over his muscular torso
and right toward those lips on the front of his tight
trunks.

At this point she really had no idea who was seducing whom, but she wondered if the battle of control would continue to volley back and forth.

"How was the water?" she asked.

"Refreshing." He glanced down toward the drinks. "Did you take mine, too?"

She rolled back to her stomach and put her mouth on the straw in lieu of an answer. Kelly flipped a page in her book, though she wasn't even focused on the actual words. She needed something to do with her shaky hands.

"I'll go get us more drinks," he told her.

"No need." She still kept her attention on her book as if everything in their little world hadn't exploded an hour ago. "I already asked for another round. The butler came by a minute ago."

"Will I be able to have my own drink this time?"

Kelly closed her book, grabbed the piña colada from the holder on the bed, and turned to sit up and face Luke. She smiled, though nerves danced in her belly at so many unknowns that would be facing them in the next few days.

"I ordered doubles, so you will get your own."

"How much do you plan on drinking?" he asked.

She shrugged. "Considering I'm on vacation, who knows. I do love a good fruity cocktail, though. I might have some wine with dinner. But don't worry, I'm also getting plenty of water."

Swinging her legs over the side of the bed, she

came to her feet and held onto her almost-empty drink. "Were you concerned for me, Luke?"

"I just don't want you getting dehydrated."

She laughed. "Whatever you say. Lunch is also being delivered in about an hour, so if you want to swim or just relax here go ahead. I plan on heading to the ocean to cool off."

As she spoke, his eyes would dip to her body, then back up to her face. The man was fighting with his willpower, and she couldn't wait for him to cave and just take what he wanted. There was no way, from that red-hot kiss, that he didn't want her.

Honestly, she wasn't looking for some ring on her finger or happily-ever-after. Oh, she was attracted to his intelligence, his determination, his compassion for those he cared for.

But the man fueled literally every one of her fantasies. Dates she'd gone on over the years just didn't compare to Luke…not that she'd ever tell him that. His ego was growing by the minute and didn't need more help.

As she started by him, he reached for her arm and stopped her.

"You've intrigued me," he murmured. "I don't know what the hell to do about this. I'm still processing everything."

He eased her around so she faced him fully. She stumbled in the sand and threw her hands up. They landed on his chest, and he steadied her with both hands on her upper arms. She had no choice but to stare up at him as he loomed over her with that hard, wet body pressed to hers.

"The ball might have been in your court all this time," he murmured. "But now that I know the truth, I'm in control."

The way he delivered that delicious threat had her body heating up in anticipation and arousal.

"Sounds like fun," she replied with a smile. "Can't wait to see what you come up with."

Kelly pulled from his grasp and made her way to the ocean, knowing full well Luke's gaze was firmly planted on her ass.

"I think we need to focus on investors for our overseas resorts."

Kelly glanced across the patio table as Luke cut into his baked fish and attempted to discuss business. Seriously? Her body had been about to go up in flames all day and he was trying to talk shop?

"Save it for the boardroom." She stabbed one of her fresh pieces of pineapple and popped it in her mouth. "No work while we're on vacation."

His eyes met hers across the small round table. "That's the only way of life I know."

Kelly dropped her fork and curled her hand around her glass of sweet tea. "Luke, you honestly need a hobby or something to take your mind off work."

"Your kiss took my mind off work," he tossed

back. "That damn strappy suit took my mind off work."

"Glad I could help," she joked with a smile. "Let me know anytime you want to be distracted again."

Luke sighed and eased back in his seat. He still hadn't put a shirt on, but she'd thrown on her wrap cover-up. Still, sitting here having a meal while barely dressed was a level of intimacy she'd never shared with him before.

"You think this is a good idea?" he asked gruffly.

"Whether it's a good idea or not is irrelevant," she countered. "That doesn't change the sexual tension between us."

"There shouldn't be any," he snarled.

Kelly couldn't tell if he was angry with himself for being turned on or if he was upset that he hadn't noticed before.

"I know you've had me in this nice little assistant box for a long time, but it's okay to move those boxes around."

He continued to stare at her, those dark, penetrating eyes seeming to go almost black. Oh, he was aroused and not happy about it. That delighted her more than she thought possible because that smoldering passion was no doubt going to explode, and she planned on being right here to enjoy it.

"I don't like change," he told her. "I don't have time for it. I have a company to save and a family that is counting on me."

Kelly laughed. "No wonder you're cranky. You don't make time for fun because it's not work."

"I have fun," he defended.

"Doing what?"

He shrugged. "I do things."

Kelly crossed her arms and pursed her lips. "Buying new cars or upgrading your jet doesn't count."

"Funny," he mocked. "For your information, I enjoy working out and running marathons."

That was news to her. Well, not the working out part. A man didn't get a sculpted body like that without putting in the time and effort. But she truly had no idea about the marathons.

"I've worked for you for five years and I'm just now learning about these marathons?"

Luke shrugged. "Should I come to work and display my medals in my office?"

No, he would never do something like that. When Luke Holloway was at work, his mind was solely on the job. But he'd never been one to brag which made him all the more attractive.

"So how many marathons have you done?" she asked.

"A few."

Kelly snorted. "Oh, please. What's the number? You have your spreadsheets memorized, so you know how many marathons you've run."

"Forty-seven."

Her eyes went wide at that number. She was expecting him to say like five or even ten. But forty-seven? Good heavens.

"That's quite remarkable," she told him. "I assure you, if I ran forty-seven marathons, I'd sure as hell be hanging up those medals. The only thing I run for is the coffee pot first thing in the morning."

Luke eased back up and went back to his lunch. "Running is therapeutic for me."

"I'm ashamed to admit, I don't work out." She took another sip of her tea and grabbed her fork. "I try to offset that by eating somewhat healthy."

"Your body is just fine."

She glanced across the table to see his eyes firmly on hers. There went those butterflies once again. How could she have schoolgirl giddiness and very adult fantasies all rolled together?

Anticipation. That was the only explanation. She had no clue what was going to happen here and that level of the unknown might be just as thrilling as anything else.

"Speaking of bodies, our massages are scheduled soon." Kelly sat her cloth napkin on the table and eased her chair back as she came to her feet. "I'm going to go rinse off in the shower to make sure all the sand and sunscreen are off."

He sat back in his seat, looking all relaxed and sexy. "I don't really need—"

Kelly held up her hands. "Stop right there. You

are getting a massage. You will love it and you will thank me afterward. End of discussion."

His lips quirked. "Yes, ma'am."

Oh, she could get used to those words coming out of his mouth. She nodded her silent thanks and turned to head to the shower. Although she could have invited him to join her, she rather liked this sexual tension and naughty flirting. She also wanted him to make the next move. Kelly had laid out her feelings. Luke knew full well where she stood, so the ball was in his court.

But, that didn't mean he held all the power here.

Kelly made her way into her bathroom and stripped down as she stepped into the large open shower with the rain head. She fully intended to hold tight on the reins of control during this trip. However, she couldn't let her heart get involved, not with knowing Luke was cut from the same cloth as her father. Both workaholics with no time for anything else.

When Kelly entered into a serious relationship, she wouldn't settle for less than being first in her partner's life.

But, she wasn't going to turn down a fling with the one man she'd been fantasizing about for years. This was the chance she'd been waiting on.

Nine

Luke didn't do massages. He didn't do facials or pedicures, or any other spa, self-care nonsense. How did people make time for this? His mode of relaxing was running, and that was when his work schedule allowed.

He felt like he was on display here. Nobody had warned him he'd be bare-ass naked with only a thin towel covering his backside.

Kelly lay on the table next to him on the beach. Which, thankfully, provided a delicious distraction from his cringe-worthy state of undress. And he grudgingly conceded that the sound of the ocean waves in the background did have some of the tension leaving his body…or at least some of his work tension.

The sexual frustration was practically exploding all around him because, every now and then, Kelly would let out the softest moan and his entire body would tighten with a need he shouldn't have for his assistant. He had to think of something else, *anything* else, before he embarrassed himself when he turned over to lay on his back. That towel wasn't going to be able to conceal anything.

Kelly might have told him not to discuss work, but that wouldn't stop him from thinking about it and all the ways he could potentially jumpstart Wingate.

That would definitely keep his hormones in check because there was nothing about this situation that was enticing. He carried the weight around everywhere, desperately seeking the answers to bring the company into the next phase of their future projections.

He sighed. Their loyal employees were counting on him; his brothers and aunt were, too. Granted, his family was also involved and everyone was working like never before to make this black cloud disappear. But with Luke being VP of New Product Development, he shouldered the majority of the responsibility.

Ava had taken him in when his parents had died and there was a large part of him that felt obligated to take this burden from her. She'd been through so much and she deserved to be cared for, to be protected from all of this.

The masseuse dug into that crook between his neck and his shoulder, and Luke nearly moaned himself. As much as he'd been against getting a massage, those hands were magical.

An instant image of Kelly running her hands all over his body instantly popped into his mind. He wouldn't mind giving her a rubdown as well.

Damn it. He was supposed to be concentrating on anything other than Kelly and that body she kept displaying.

She was more than just sexy curves, though. That did not even *begin* to scratch the surface of what this woman was made of. He'd always known how intelligent and astute she was, and to that end, he never went into a meeting without her. Heck, his assistant was like the second half of his brain. If there was something he didn't think of, he knew she would. Many times she was already ahead of him and he'd never had to ask her to do anything twice.

But it wasn't until yesterday that he discovered just how persistent, demanding, and strong-willed she could be. All of that combined was too damn sexy and he was having a difficult time resisting her.

He *should* be resisting her. She worked for him, after all, and he had to keep reminding himself that if they entered into a fling and it ended badly, then what would happen? He couldn't risk losing her as an assistant or a friend. She'd been there for him through so much and there weren't many people he trusted. He had to keep everyone in those labeled boxes like she'd mentioned. Moving anything around would completely throw off his entire life.

"You can roll to your back now," the masseuse whispered into his ear.

She lifted the towel slightly as he turned to his back. Next to him, he caught sight of Kelly rolling over as well. That glimpse of side breast was seriously not helping him keep his hormones in check.

And this massage was doing the opposite of relaxing him. If anything, he was more revved up than ever. He wanted her in the worst possible way but, for all the reasons he'd just listed to himself, having sex with Kelly Prentiss was a horrible idea.

Maybe he should think about Christmas instead. Less than a month away and he still needed to get Kelly something. He was so bad at this. For the past five years, he'd given her a hefty bonus. Even when the company was plummeting, he'd given her money from his personal account. She was too invaluable to not show his appreciation.

Yet now…now everything had changed and he was absolutely clueless.

Luke focused on breathing slowly, trying to get his mind to calm down from going a hundred different directions. However, trying not to think about

Kelly next to him wearing nothing but these damn towels? Well, that proved nearly impossible.

But, regardless, he *had* to stay strong because too much was at stake. They still had four days here, and somehow, someway, he was going to have to muster some serious willpower to resist her seductive charms.

The massage was absolutely fabulous. Kelly finally felt relaxed and ready to tackle anything.

The masseuses left them alone on the beach to dress in private. She smiled, knowing the ladies had just assumed she and Luke were a couple. There was really no need to explain otherwise.

Kelly swung her legs over the side of the cabana and reached for her cover-up. She slid the simple black sheath over her head and came to her feet.

When she glanced back, Luke was laying on his side staring up at her. Between that little towel covering his most essential parts and his skin glistening from the oils used during the massage, Kelly had to pull in a deep breath to calm herself. Gah! Even having normal thoughts around him was starting to become difficult.

"What do you have planned now?" he asked.

That low, husky voice reminded her of her fantasies. She knew full well what that voice would sound like in the dark as his body slid over hers beneath the sheets.

"Is there something you want to do?" she asked.

That naughty grin had her smiling right back at him.

"I know, that was a loaded question," she said before he could comment. "Dinner won't be for several hours still. We can always rent a car and drive around the island, or we could hang here and continue relaxing without thinking of work."

Luke's eyes raked over her, something he kept doing lately, and she didn't miss that hunger staring back at her. Was he about to suggest they go back to the room? Or maybe he'd tell her to lay back down with him, as they had their own private beach and she'd paid for total privacy.

She wanted him now more than ever. And the best part was that she knew the feeling was mutual. He'd been eyeing her for days and there was no longer a doubt in her mind that he craved her with just as much fervor as she craved him.

Even so, she assumed Luke was still battling between his professional and personal life—not wanting to mix the two considering their positions. She hoped like hell this was the one time he'd put his work mode on hold to go after what he wanted... She was banking on that.

"Exploring the island might be the best," he told her gruffly. "Staying here alone isn't the smartest idea."

Oh, she thought it was a *fabulous* idea, but she was also up for a little exploration.

"I'll go get ready and meet you in about thirty minutes," she said. "I know just where we should go."

He continued to hold her gaze. "You're not taking me to a nude beach, are you?"

"Now why would I do that when we could get nude on our own private beach?" she volleyed back with a smile. "It's a surprise, so go get ready."

"I'm starting to become afraid of your surprises."

Kelly laughed. "I just like to keep you on your toes."

Turning away before he could comment, she headed up the beach toward their bungalow. She'd done enough research online and made some calls in advance to learn the areas to explore that would be private and dodge all the tourist hot spots. After all, she still wanted this time for Luke to be relaxing, and she really didn't want to be around a bunch of people.

Kelly quickly showered and pulled her hair into a top knot. She threw on her black bikini, a pair of cut-off jean shorts, and a white tank. Then she slid on her canvas shoes, tossed some necessities into her beach bag, and checked her cell to make sure the car was ready and out front.

Zeke had left instructions with the owner to ensure the staff knew Kelly was in charge and anything she wanted would be at her disposal. She appreciated that, she truly did, but she couldn't imagine what all of this was costing him.

She'd come to realize that it paid to have money and people on standby.

There was nothing she wouldn't do for Luke and lying to get him here was something she would never regret…no matter how things turned out. Yes, she wanted him to cleanse his mind and get a fresh start back at work, but she wanted him to see her as more than his assistant and sometimes buddy. She wanted him to see her the way she'd seen him all these years.

With each passing moment, that was becoming a very real reality. Something was developing between them and she wasn't sure if this was just a physical bond or whether there was more. The anticipation was part of the thrill and she couldn't wait to see what today brought them.

But…the more she learned about Luke on a personal level, the more she wondered how difficult it would be to keep her heart out of the equation.

Kelly stepped out of her bedroom to find him waiting in the living area. He glanced up from his spot on the couch and came to his feet. She couldn't help but laugh.

"Another new outfit," she stated with a nod. "I hope you're going to sport some of this snazzy wardrobe back at the office."

He glanced down to the T-shirt that read "Don't Worry—Beach Happy" and the bright pink shorts.

"These clothes will never make it back to Texas," he growled.

"Aw, now you know that shirt would be a big hit at the next board meeting," she told him. "Why be so predictable with a suit and tie?"

He glared at her. "Because I'm the VP and nothing about this is professional."

"But it's fun. Remember that word?"

Luke blew out a sigh and started toward the door. "You keep reminding me."

Kelly shoved her cell into the bag on her shoulder and stepped out of the bungalow. The warm afternoon sun fell on her face and she was so excited to spend the day frolicking with Luke without a care in the world. Her greatest fantasy was coming to life and, for now, she was going to enjoy the moment and not worry about what would happen once they left this paradise.

As they made their way to the front of the resort, a bellman greeted them and opened the doors to the white Jeep that awaited them.

"How the hell did you get a vehicle this fast?" Luke muttered as they got closer.

"Stick with me and you'll have all the fun things in life." She sent him a wink. "Just kidding. Zeke left his card and said I was to use it as I saw fit."

Kelly circled the hood and jumped into the driver's seat, thanking the resort employee for his help. When Luke settled in beside her, he turned to her.

"Where are you taking me?" he asked.

She put the Jeep in gear, so glad they had given her one with the top off, and adjusted her sunglasses.

"You trust me?" she asked.

Luke merely chuckled as she tore off out of the resort, heading for their day of fun.

Ten

Luke admired the beautiful scenery as Kelly maneuvered through the streets. The fresh air was a welcome reminder that he needed to get out of the office more. Lately, his usual days were spent heading into work early and going home late.

He tried to grab a run before or after the office at least four days a week, but sometimes that just wasn't possible. On occasion, a very *rare* occasion, he'd get to the Texas Cattleman's Club for an evening of drinking and darts with some friends. But lately those nights had been so few and far between.

Luke didn't have time for fun and he sure as hell didn't have time to be on vacation. But, he couldn't ignore that the longer he was here, the more he was okay with the fact Kelly had conspired with his brother and kidnapped him.

There was still that guilt that seemed to have settled in deep. The guilt for being away from the office, the guilt for enjoying the hell out of this flirtation with Kelly, and the guilt that he still hadn't found a way to save Wingate.

Luke glanced from the picturesque blue water to the woman in the driver's seat. That glorious red hair blew all around her shoulders and face. She drove with a smile as she tapped her fingers on the steering wheel as if she had a steady beat in her head. He'd never seen her so calm, so free and spirited.

Something shifted inside of him. Something he couldn't quite put his finger on. All he knew was there was so much more to Kelly than he'd ever realized. She was more playful, more alive, and vibrant…and a hell of a lot sexier than he'd ever imagined.

She hadn't a care in the world right now. In the office, she was always on top of everything, her mind often worked like his and they were always in sync. Now though, she had clearly pushed Wingate aside and was solely in the present. Part of him envied her that she could compartmentalize her life in such a way.

Kelly loved Wingate just as much as he did, so it wasn't that she didn't take her job seriously. Her title might be assistant, but she really was so much more. She busted her ass to make him look good in front of potential investors. Her spreadsheets and slideshows were spot on for each board meeting and he was always proud to give her the due credit she deserved.

In the distance behind Kelly, the mountains peaked. There was something extremely calming about Oahu. He'd never been before and any time he traveled, he never did so for pleasure, or even with a female companion.

Everything about this trip was foreign to him. How could he ignore these strong, albeit brand new, emotions he was having for Kelly? Was it smart to even think about acting on them? They were just so damn potent, but he had to wonder if that was because they were alone on a tropical island that just screamed romance and sex.

Romance and *sex* were definitely two words he had never associated with her, but they were all he could think about now.

What started out as a crazy plan from his brother had quickly morphed into an incredible adventure. How could he not enjoy himself here with Kelly? Maybe if he made more time for decompressing, he'd be at the top of his game.

Kelly tried tucking her hair behind her ears, but the wind continued to whip it about. He had a sudden image of that hair sliding over his body as her mouth explored him and his tacky shorts just got a bit tighter.

Kelly pulled onto a narrow road leading away from the ocean. He wanted to ask again where they were going, but he knew she wouldn't tell him. She was having way too much fun with all of these surprises and, other than the terrible wardrobe, he was having a pretty good time. That massage had been amazing and the food had been incredible.

When she pulled the Jeep over on the side of the road and killed the engine, he glanced around to the base of the mountains and the rocky area surrounding them.

"We're here?" he asked.

Kelly climbed out of the vehicle and grabbed her bag from the back. "We are. Let's go."

He didn't know where they were heading, but he obliged and followed her. He wasn't one to typically take orders, but again, he couldn't deny this was part of the appeal of Kelly and this impromptu trip.

The rushing water seemed to echo off the rocks. He heard before he saw, but as soon as they walked a little farther and rounded the bend, Kelly stopped and gasped.

"It's even more breathtaking than they said," she murmured.

Luke came up beside her and stared at the rushing waterfall as it flowed into the crisp blue water below. It seemed so far away, yet still close enough to touch.

"I was given a tip about this place," she told him, her eyes still locked onto nature's beauty. "It's a waterfall only the locals know about and it's usually pretty private."

She started toward the path that would take them down to the base and Luke set out behind her. Beyond the beauty of this place that amazed him, he was also stunned at all the trouble she'd gone to now that they were here. Zeke might have footed the bill, something Luke would discuss when he got back, but Kelly had planned all the fun. This was only their first full day in Oahu and he had no idea what else she had in store.

Once they reached the bottom, Kelly sat her bag on the ground and toed off her shoes. When she slid that tank overhead, leaving her in only short denim shorts and a triangle bikini top, Luke had to fight back the urge to grab her and see if those kisses from earlier were still just as hot and arousing as he remembered.

"Want to get in?" she asked, that voice and smile so damn tempting.

"You didn't tell me to wear a suit."

Her eyes widened. "I didn't? Oops."

She unbuttoned her shorts, and he watched as they slid down her tanned legs and she kicked them aside. She stood there in her black bikini that looked like the other one that drove him insane. So much skin practically begging for him to explore with his hands and his mouth.

"Maybe you could jump in with your boxer briefs," she suggested. "They'd be no different than the trunks you have."

He took a step toward her, then another, until they were toe to toe. She tipped her head up to keep him in her sights.

"I'm not wearing any underwear," he told her.

Her face tinged a pretty little pink and, for the first time since he'd known her, she'd gone speechless.

"Well, then…" she stammered. "You can just, uh, I guess you can go skinny dipping. Nobody is here."

Luke took a step back and reached for the button on his shorts. Her eyes locked right onto his hands and that hunger and desire he saw had lust pumping through him. He couldn't exactly act on his attraction here in the open. Granted they were secluded, but anyone could come down at any time.

Luke decided since she'd teased the hell out of him, he'd turn the tables. He released the button and reached behind his back to grab a fistful of his T-shirt. He tossed it to the ground and couldn't help but swell with pride as her bright eyes traveled all over his bare torso.

He shouldn't be relishing in having his assistant look at him like he was everything she'd been starving for, but he couldn't deny that he wanted those eyes on him. He wanted her hands and her mouth on him, too. Damn it all…he wanted her and everything about that was completely wrong.

What would his family say if he came back from this and there was a shift in the dynamics between Kelly and him? Because if they ended up having sex, nothing would ever be the same back at Wingate. Hell, he'd already done everything in his mind so how could anything ever go back to the way it was before?

When he unzipped his shorts and started easing them down, Kelly pulled in an audible breath as her eyes widened.

"You big liar," she swatted at his chest. "You wore underwear."

"Oh, did I?" he asked. "Oops."

She continued to grin as he tossed her joke back in her face, but she still had that passion heavy in her eyes.

"Race you," she called a second before she took off toward the water.

Luke had barely gotten out of his shorts before he was issued the challenge and took off after her. She beat him by a step and he was surprised how warm the water was as it lapped up around them.

Kelly continued to laugh as she dipped her body down and came back up. He'd never been so jealous of water droplets in all of his life. They ran over her bare shoulders, they ran between her breasts, they ran down her abdomen. Everywhere he saw a trail of water, he wanted to lick it.

"This feels amazing," she exclaimed. "I'm so glad I found out about this."

She had to nearly shout because the waterfall echoed. He'd traveled all over the globe for business, but he'd never seen a more beautiful sight than Kelly with all that wet, bare skin with the most spectacular waterfall in the background.

The water came to his waist, but he made his way deeper to where she stood. As he approached her, her breathing seemed to come out in pants and those green eyes mesmerized him in a way he'd never been before.

This was Kelly. His Kelly. The woman who spent more time with him than any other woman ever. Even when he'd been engaged, Luke still spent the bulk of his days at the office—something his ex never could understand.

Luke didn't reach for Kelly, but the way the force of the water kept rushing against them, there was no way to prevent their bodies from rocking against each other.

"You seem relaxed." She reached up and smoothed her fingertip down the space between his brows. "No worry lines. That's a first for you."

That simple touch snapped the very last bit of willpower he had. Luke took her hand and flattened her palm against his chest as he rested his free hand against the curve of her hip. He gripped her, pulling her pelvis closer to his.

The tips of her fingers dug into his chest and she tipped her head just enough for him to lean down and feather his lips across hers.

With their bare torsos suctioned together by the water, their hips held together from his grip, Luke wanted more.

He opened his mouth and covered hers, taking what he wanted and damning the consequences. She opened for him just like before only this time he knew what to expect. He knew how hard this punch of desire would hit him and how he might never recover from such an impact.

Kelly slid her hand up to his shoulder and around the back of his head. She gripped his hair and gave a slight tug, only adding to his arousal. He never knew how much an assertive woman would turn him on, but she'd shown that her ability to take control in any situation was damn attractive.

Luke reached around, grabbing her entire backside and lifting her body against his. Kelly wrapped her legs around him, grinding her hips, silently begging for more.

They were out in the open. At any given moment, another couple, a family, hell an entire tour group could start coming down, and he didn't care. He wanted Kelly with a fierceness he didn't even recognize within himself.

"Luke."

Even over the roar of the waterfall he heard her panting his name. Considering he wasn't used to her in this capacity, the newness of everything had him desperate for more, had him wondering how soon they could get back to their private bungalow where he could show her exactly what he wanted to do to her.

"Not here," he murmured against her lips. "I want you, Kelly. Just…not here."

She eased back, those bright eyes sparking with desire. "You can't tell me that and then put the brakes on. I've wanted you too long, Luke."

She was right. He couldn't imagine the need she'd had for so long. He'd only just come into these overwhelming emotions and she deserved to at least have the edge taken off. Luke wasn't so sure he could wait either, but he would for her. He wanted her in bed and in private, where he could show her exactly how much he hungered for her.

With one arm banded around her waist, Luke used his free hand to slide between their bodies. He grazed his fingertip along the elastic at the curve on the inside of her hip, causing those hips to jerk again.

She settled into his touch, wrapping her arms around his neck and resting her forehead against his. When he eased his finger beneath the edge of her bottoms, Kelly let out a cry and nothing could

"One Minute" Survey

You get up to **FOUR books** <u>and</u> TWO Mystery Gifts...

> ## ABSOLUTELY FREE!

Sizzling Romance

YOU pick your books – WE pay for everything!

Passionate Romance

See inside for details.

YOU pick your books –
WE pay for everything.
You get up to FOUR new books and TWO Mystery Gifts
absolutely FREE!
Total retail value: Over $20!

Dear Reader,

Your opinions are important to us. So if you'll participate in our fast
and free "One Minute" Survey, **YOU** can pick up to four wonderful
books that **WE** pay for!

As a leading publisher of women's fiction, we'd love to hear from
you. That's why we promise to reward you for completing our
survey.

IMPORTANT: Please complete the survey and return it. We'll send
your Free Books and Free Mystery Gifts right away. **And we pay
for shipping and handling too!** ← *We pay for EVERYTHING!*

Try **Harlequin® Desire** books featuring the worlds of the
American elite with juicy plot twists, delicious sensuality and
intriguing scandal.

Try **Harlequin Presents® Larger-Print** books featuring the
glamourous lives of royals and billionaires in a world of exotic
locations, where passion knows no bounds.

Or TRY BOTH!

Thank you again for participating in our "One Minute"
Survey. It really takes just a minute (or less) to complete the
survey… and your free books and gifts will be well worth it!

Sincerely,

Pam Powers

Pam Powers
for Reader Service

"One Minute" Survey

GET YOUR FREE BOOKS AND FREE GIFTS!

✓ Complete this Survey   ✓ Return this survey

▶ DETACH AND MAIL CARD TODAY! ▶

1 Do you try to find time to read every day?
☐ YES   ☐ NO

2 Do you prefer stories with happy endings?
☐ YES   ☐ NO

3 Do you enjoy having books delivered to your home?
☐ YES   ☐ NO

4 Do you find a Larger Print size easier on your eyes?
☐ YES   ☐ NO

YES! I have completed the above "One Minute" Survey. Please send me my Free Books and Free Mystery Gifts (worth over $20 retail). I understand that I am under no obligation to buy anything, as explained on the back of this card.

☐ I prefer Harlequin® Desire 225/326 HDL GNWS
☐ I prefer Harlequin Presents® Larger Print 176 /376 HDL GNWS
☐ I prefer BOTH 225/326 & 176/376 HDL GNW4

FIRST NAME   LAST NAME

ADDRESS

APT.#   CITY

STATE/PROV.   ZIP/POSTAL CODE

stop him from pleasuring her now. He wanted to take all of her passion, he wanted to *own* it.

Luke eased his finger into her, gritting his teeth as his own arousal continued to spike. This was all for Kelly, though. Later, he vowed, later they would take their time and explore each other.

Suddenly all those reasons this was a bad idea completely vanished from his mind. Nothing mattered except Kelly and giving her everything she wanted, everything she'd been waiting for.

He continued to pleasure her, sliding his thumb over her core to add even more to her experience. He wanted this to be perfect for her, he wanted to be remembered and branded in her mind forever.

How the hell had he come to this? Kelly was too damn powerful with this invisible hold she had over him. Damn it, he wanted her more than his next breath, and he wished like hell they would have stayed back at their beach house.

Her body jerked faster as he continued to touch her in just the right spot. Getting to know her body in such an intimate way wasn't something he ever expected…and now he didn't know how he could do without.

Kelly continued to cling to him as the wave of pleasure overcame her. Luke continued to work his hand against her, drawing out every bit of ecstasy. There was so much more he wanted to show her, to *give* her, but this would have to do for now.

When her body calmed, Kelly eased back and stared into his eyes.

"Luke, I—"

He quickly cut her words off with a kiss, then pulled back.

"No words," he rasped. "Whatever is happening here, we just need to let it happen."

He never thought those words would come out of his mouth, but this woman had changed so much within him in such a short time.

Kelly pulled in a shaky breath and shook her head. She unhooked her legs from his waist and smoothed her hair from her face.

"Fine," she breathed. "But just know when we get back to the bungalow, I plan on returning the favor."

And with that wicked promise she dove under the water and took off swimming toward the waterfall.

Eleven

Kelly's body tingled the entire rest of the day. Once they left the waterfall, she ended up driving them around the island, hitting some local shops to buy trinkets she didn't need. She'd never expected to have had such a memorable day.

From the waterfall in Luke's arms to traveling around an exotic location with a man she was falling for, she couldn't imagine what else was in store for them the rest of their days here.

Kelly sighed. She didn't *want* to be falling for him—she had initially thought she could keep her heart out of this equation. But apparently some things were beyond her control. Even so, there were still too many parallels between Luke and her father. Kelly had seen the way her mother had suffered, vying for the attention of the man she loved. Kelly always vowed she would never let herself get into such a position.

She had to keep reminding herself that she couldn't hinge a life after this with Luke. He would go back to his job and she would go back to being his assistant. There would be no happily-ever-after or ring on her finger. And she was okay with that. This was her greatest fantasy and she would ignore the reality that awaited them when they returned to Texas.

Once they were back at the resort and headed toward their bungalow, the anticipation continued to build even higher, faster. Kelly wanted him out of those silly clothes and she wanted to explore every delicious inch of his body.

Luke stepped up to their door and punched in the code. As soon as they stepped inside, she noticed their dinner had been delivered and was set up out on the patio. The cart with everything extra sat in their dining area. There were rose petals leading from the front door, down in the sunken living area, and on out to the patio, circling the table.

She certainly hadn't told the resort that this was a romantic getaway. She knew Zeke had tipped heavily in advance for extra privacy, to keep the drinks and snacks always stocked, and only notify her if they needed anything. She didn't want Luke interrupted by anything or to be distracted by any outside issues…hence the electronics ban.

"I didn't realize we were gone so long," she told him.

Kelly went to take her shopping bags to her room. When she came back out, Luke still remained by the front door, but his eyes were solely on her. And there it was. She had hoped that hunger in his eyes back at the waterfall wasn't just because he'd pleasured her and that he fully intended to fulfill his promise that they would pick up where they'd left off once they returned.

And apparently that wish was not for naught.

"Do you want to go eat?" she asked.

Luke stripped that shirt off once again. She would never tire of seeing that magnificent physique on display. There was so much to take in, so much to admire and appreciate. Starting with that dark chest hair splattered over his smooth, satiny skin and trailing down to his ripped abs. And *hot damn*! Where had that dragon tattoo, which covered his entire back with a portion coming around his side, come from?

She'd never seen his ink before, and he'd never talked about it. Now she was even more curious about the man she'd been intrigued with for years.

"Dinner can wait."

Luke stalked toward her like a panther to his prey and Kelly took a step back. The closer he got, the more she eased back, excited for the thrill of the

chase. She'd never guess he would be this commanding, this *primal*. The way he looked at her with a
need so intense, she couldn't wait to fulfill his every
fantasy.

Fantasy…that was the word she had to keep focusing on because that would certainly keep her heart
protected. Nothing about this was real and nothing
would be long-term.

When her back hit the wall next to her bedroom
door, Luke came right up against her, resting one
hand on the side of her head and then caging her in
with the other hand.

That bare, muscular chest kept rubbing against her
tank, and she wished he'd strip her out of her clothes.
She wanted to feel him against her like she had at the
waterfall. There was nothing stopping them now, no
chance of being interrupted or seen.

Luke's dark eyes remained locked onto hers as
he eased one hand between them. He never looked
away from her as he jerked the snap on her shorts.
Kelly reached down and shifted her hips from side
to side as she wiggled out of them. When the shorts
fell to her ankles, she kicked them aside.

Smiling with pure male satisfaction, Luke gripped
the hem of her tank and jerked it up and over her
head, leaving her in only her bikini and him in his
black boxer briefs.

Exchanging a few heated kisses in the waterfall
was one thing, but what was about to happen now

was entirely different. He'd never seen her completely naked and vice versa. She wanted those briefs gone. She wanted to fulfill her promise of returning the sexual favor.

Kelly had waited so long for this and, as much as she wanted to hurry and get to the good stuff, she also wanted to take her time and relish every single moment and every single touch.

She arched to reach behind her back to undo the strings of her bikini top, but Luke beat her to it. He had those knots ripped away in record time. The garment fell between them, leaving her entire chest exposed. Then he did the same to the strings along her hips.

Suddenly, she stood before him completely naked and more turned on than she could ever remember. Luke took one step back, his eyes raking over her from head to toe. He made no apologies or excuses; in fact, he said nothing as he took in all of her in her most vulnerable state.

And Kelly didn't mind one bit. She wanted him to look. She wasn't shy of her body and, from the hunger in his eyes, Luke most definitely liked what he saw.

"Take them off," she ordered, nodding to his briefs.

With a crooked, naughty grin, he continued to stare back at her as he hooked his thumbs in his waistband and shoved the briefs to the floor. He kicked them aside and merely stood there with his hands on his hips.

If she looked as chiseled and perfect as Luke, she'd go around parading her body, too. Suddenly, she didn't feel so confident about her own.

Kelly started to cross her arms, but Luke stepped forward and gripped her wrists. He held her arms out wide and left plenty of room between them so he could see her entire body.

"Never hide from me," he commanded. "Nothing this beautiful should ever be hidden. You deserve to be explored, to be treasured."

Kelly swallowed, unsure of what happened to make him switch from putting a stop to this, to suddenly wanting everything she was willing to give.

"I didn't expect you to be so…" She knew she sounded ridiculous and likely her cheeks were flushed. "Perfect and well-toned."

"While I appreciate that, I want you to know that this body of yours has driven me out of my mind," he admitted. "Someone who wears a thong in front of her boss shouldn't be embarrassed to be naked."

She smiled and shook her head. "It's not that I'm embarrassed, per se, but I guess I just want to be everything you want…if that makes sense."

He pulled her hands to his chest and stepped against her, trapping their joined hands.

"You are everything I want right now."

Right now. Another reminder of how temporary all of this was.

"I guess I'm nervous," she admitted. "I've wanted you for so long, I just—"

Luke cut her off with his mouth on hers. Kelly opened for him, glad he'd taken control because she didn't want to think, she only wanted to *feel* and to return this passion he offered.

He lifted her against him, as he'd done at the waterfall, and she locked her ankles behind his back as he carried her into his bedroom.

Suddenly she was being tipped backward, and she landed on his soft bed. Luke went down with her, his weight pressing into hers on the mattress. His arousal settled perfectly between her thighs and she had to muster all of her willpower to not cry out.

The waterfall climax had taken some of the edge off, but she wanted so much more. She wanted to explore him and take their time. She wanted to know what made Luke come undone…and she wanted to see him lose control because of her touch.

"Do you have protection?" she whispered against his lips.

Luke eased back and shook his head. "I wasn't planning on this when we left."

"I have condoms," she admitted. "I *was* planning on this."

His eyes seemed to grow darker. "Where are they?"

"My room. In the drawer of the nightstand."

Then he was up and off of her. Kelly glanced out the patio door to the ocean and drank in the backdrop of the orange sunset. This was really going to happen, and she couldn't wait.

Her focus shifted back to the bedroom door when Luke stepped in fully naked and wearing the protection. The way he crossed the room to climb back up onto the bed had her sitting up on her elbows and pulling her knees up, ready for him to settle back where he'd just been.

"You look so damn sexy," he said as he loomed above her.

His hand went between her legs and Kelly bit her lip as intense pleasure pulsated within her. Then that touch vanished a second before he gripped the sensitive spot behind her knees and jerked her legs back even farther.

She kept her gaze locked onto his as Luke joined their bodies. There was no way to keep from crying out and arching against the glorious sensation.

With her legs dangling over his arms, Kelly reached out to grip his biceps. The muscles strained beneath her touch as Luke continued to work his hips against hers.

She couldn't control her moans and sighs, not when this felt so good and even more intense than she'd ever fantasized about.

Luke gripped her backside, lifting her farther into

him as he increased the pace. This new position completely undid Kelly as her climax overcame her. She dug her fingers into his arms and called his name, begging him not to stop, begging him for more.

She knew he followed her in his own release with the way he'd stilled and held her so tight, like he never wanted to let her go.

Luke stayed with her until his body stopped trembling and then he slowly released her legs and came down to lie half on her, half on the bed. With one long leg and one strong arm draped across her, she'd never felt more protected or cherished. Yes, this was just sex, but to her this moment was so much more....

Kelly kept her eyes closed as if she could remain in this euphoria forever. Opening her eyes would bring back the reality that they weren't on this romantic getaway as a real couple. Rather, they were here because she'd tricked him.

She wasn't contrite, though. Luke needed the break and she'd wanted to see if they could be more. She couldn't be sorry for going after what she wanted.

His warm breath fell on her shoulder, sending even more tingles through her body. The low hum of the large fan suspended from the peaked ceiling relaxed her and settled her nerves. While she'd always wanted this to happen, she was never sure it actually would, and she certainly hadn't planned for how to react after.

"Should we go eat now?" he murmured against her shoulder.

Kelly was relieved he was the one to break the silence. She trailed her fingers up and down his arm across her chest.

"I'm in no hurry to get out of this bed," she answered honestly.

Luke came up on his elbow and glanced down at her. Those dark, heavy-lidded eyes had gone all soft and sexy. She wondered what he was thinking, but she wasn't going to be that woman who wanted to have postcoital chat sessions. She didn't need reassurance that he enjoyed himself or that he wasn't having regrets. She knew Luke enough to know that he wasn't ready to run out the door.

"How about I bring dinner in here?" he suggested.

Having dinner in bed with Luke sounded like a dream, but she couldn't let herself get too wrapped up in this fantasy world. Because as much as she wanted this to be reality, Kelly also had to use her head here.

"Let's eat outside," she told him. "It's so beautiful here, I want to take advantage of it before we go back to Royal."

His lips quirked into a grin. "And here I thought you just wanted to take advantage of me."

Kelly couldn't help but laugh. "I think it's you who took advantage of me, remember? You stripped me as soon as we got inside."

"*You* seduced me with this trip."

She reached up and ran her fingertip along his stubbled jawline. "You've been seducing me for years," she murmured.

Luke's face sobered as he leaned in closer. "How did I miss this?" he whispered against her lips. "How did I not see you?"

He folded her into his embrace, holding her on top of him as he rolled to his back. Kelly straddled his lap and braced her hands on his chest.

"I take it dinner can wait?" she asked with a grin.

He reached up with one hand, gripping the back of her neck and pulling her down for a kiss.

Dinner would most definitely have to wait.

Twelve

"So how did you guys choose this place?" Luke asked.

Kelly sat in the cabana, staring out at the darkened ocean and the starry sky. The calm, warm breeze washed over her, and everything in her world seemed so right, so perfect.

For now, while they were in this island paradise, she was going to just live in the moment and not worry about Wingate or her job or what would happen once they returned. Nothing mattered but Luke.

Their time was running out, though, and she knew there would be no romantic evenings after this trip. Her boss would go back to diving headfirst into work and ignoring the rest of the world. She had to brace herself for that because this wasn't a trip designed to make him fall in love…this only started out as a means of relaxation and seduction. And while she'd taken the risk and it had paid off, there was no way she would risk her heart; that was a sure bet to lose.

Kelly glanced over her shoulder to where Luke lay reclined beside her. He wore nothing but a pair of black boxer briefs and she had on a wrap cover-up with nothing beneath. They'd eaten dinner on the patio and had come down to the cabana once the sun had already set. They had complete and utter privacy.

"Zeke found the resort and showed me one day. Once I saw the place, I was in love and started planning," she told him. "He knew you needed a break and he needed me to accompany you pretending the trip was about business. I knew this was my only chance to show you how I felt. I couldn't do it in Royal or near the office."

Luke slid his fingertips over her arm and braced his other arm behind his head. She would never tire of seeing him like this. So relaxed, so…unencumbered. The man was sexy as hell in a suit, but seeing him on a tropical island all wet and bare-chested, highlighted by the sun, did something else entirely to her.

The physical attraction had always been there, but as she'd gotten to know him, she'd appreciated his loyalty to his family. Not to mention the fact that when things got tough, he still stuck around. She'd dated a few men who fled when things got complicated instead of trying to work things out.

Stability hadn't been too strong in her personal life over the past several years. Her career was all she could cling to and Luke had always had her back. But she knew he couldn't be there on a long-term-relationship level. Luke wasn't made up like that and ultimately that's what she would need.

"This place is perfect," he agreed softly. "So… you ready to tell me why you never revealed how you feel?"

"We've already been over this," she reminded him. "The timing was never right and I couldn't take that chance."

"I never took you for someone to back down from what you wanted."

Kelly smiled and turned back to the breathtaking ocean view. She pulled her knees up in front of her and wrapped her arms around her legs.

"I did go after what I wanted," she said. "I just took my time. Patience is everything."

Luke sat up next to her, the cabana shifting with his weight. The man wasn't just formidable in the boardroom, he emanated power everywhere. All big and dominating and absolutely perfect. She couldn't find a single flaw with Luke Holloway.

"You dated while you've been employed with me,"

he murmured. "There have been flowers on your desk from time to time."

Kelly nodded. "That's true. I even dated a guy for several months about a year ago, but I was never really into them. I wanted to be. I wanted to get you out of my mind because I kept telling myself this was wrong. I mean, how cliché can I be to want to have sex with my boss? That's not professional and how would the rest of the employees react if we were... you know."

Luke's chuckle vibrated against her. "You think I'd send out an office email and inform everyone we had sex?"

"No," she laughed. "But the dynamics between us have changed and someone might pick up on that when we get back. I worry how that will look for me."

Luke reached over and slid a finger beneath her chin, turning her head to face him.

"Nobody will know a thing," he assured her gruffly. "We went away on a business trip and that's all."

Kelly really didn't know how she'd go back to work and see him in that capacity after being so intimate with him here. She knew how he tasted, how he touched and liked to be touched, what it took to make him come completely undone...

"It sounds easy enough," she agreed. "But I'm not sure I won't be able to stop—"

"From jumping me on the boardroom table?"

"No, silly!" Kelly laughed again and swatted his chest. "I was going to say I won't be able to stop from staring at you and I hope nobody picks up on that."

"Maybe I'll be the one caught staring at you," he tossed back with a grin. "Did you ever think of that?"

Kelly swallowed and shook her head. "I never thought this would actually happen. I wanted it to, but I wasn't sure you'd ever see me as more than just your assistant."

He gripped her chin between his thumb and finger again. "First of all, you have always been more than *just* an assistant. I wouldn't get anything done without you. You deserve more credit than what you give yourself."

His words warmed her deep into her heart. She knew he valued and appreciated her. Luke had always been the best boss and treated her with such respect. Even if she wasn't halfway in love with the man, she would love him simply for the way he treasured her.

"Second," he went on. "Since my engagement ended, I don't do much with dating or even looking to add someone into my life. I'm devoted to Wingate and determined to grow our product line."

"Your ex wasn't right for you."

Kelly hadn't meant to let that out, but now that she'd expressed her true feelings, she didn't care that he knew.

"Did our engagement affect how you felt?" he asked.

Kelly didn't want him to think she was looking to slip into that role of trophy fiancée. "Despite wanting you, I wasn't looking for more. I just didn't think she fit into your world. She seemed to… I don't know. Needy."

"She was," he agreed. "I'm glad I realized it before we married. I wasn't in love with her and she wanted a social status that she thought I could give her. It seemed like a good fit at first, but I seriously dodged a bullet with that one."

Marrying someone like Luke Holloway would certainly give someone a bump in their standings. It would get someone invited to the poshest parties, an automatic in with the elite Texas Cattleman's Club and money would never be an issue. Luke would give his woman everything she could ever want, and he would totally treat her like a queen.

Kelly never wanted a man to take care of her, she was more than capable of taking care of herself. She wasn't looking to marry Luke, she'd just wanted him in her bed. She wanted him to make her feel alive, to fulfill these fantasies she'd had for years.

But now that she knew they would make one hell of a team in the boardroom *and* the bedroom—it still didn't change anything. Because when it came down to it, they wanted different things out of life.

"She didn't find the work hours too appealing,"

Luke went on. "She wanted the prestige and the money, but without the work."

"Well, that's impossible, especially during crisis mode."

Luke snaked an arm around her waist and hauled her back down onto the bed. "I don't want to talk about my ex anymore," he told her brusquely.

That was something Kelly could definitely get on board with. She'd rather talk work than the woman who used to wear Luke's ring.

"I didn't even know I needed this," he stated after a minute of silence. "You were right."

Kelly snuggled deeper into his side, tucking her head just beneath his chin. "I'm always right."

His laugh vibrated against her cheek.

"What?" she asked. "I am. Where would you be without me? You've admitted you couldn't live without me in the office and now I'm right about you needing this break."

"I would have never left for anything other than meeting with an investor or finding a way to fix Wingate."

He didn't have to admit that, she knew, and that's why she had to essentially lie to him to get him on that plane. When Zeke approached her, he'd told her there would be no way his brother would meet with anyone without her by his side. He trusted her with every aspect of his business.

"I should feel guilty for deceiving you," she finally said. "But I honestly don't."

"You could have seduced me in Royal."

"As I told you before, the timing was never right." Kelly eased back and rested on her elbow to stare down at him. "And that's not the sole reason I brought you here. I really was worried about you and so was your brother."

"He's just as much of a workaholic."

"That's true," she agreed. "It's in your blood, but he does know when to take a day off here and there to give himself some space. Everyone needs to recharge at some point in time. And besides, he has Reagan."

He tucked her hair behind her ear and trailed his fingers down her cheek. Her body had never really calmed since the waterfall and now each touch and each smoldering gaze from Luke only revved her up all over again.

"How many more days do we have?" he asked.

"Three." Not long enough. "I have a fun day planned tomorrow, but if you want to stay here and be lazy and naked, I can cancel."

Luke smiled. "You've gone through so much to get everything organized and planned."

"Think of it as part of your Christmas present," she told him. "Though I didn't actually pay for anything here."

Now he did laugh. That low, rumbling laugh that she rarely heard since he was so consumed with work. She wanted more of that in her life…she wanted more of that for him.

Ugh. This couldn't be happening. She could not fall for her boss. There was no room in his life for her and she would not fall down that same loveless hole her mother did.

"I better step up my game for you," he joked. "I haven't even started shopping, but I typically get you the same thing each year."

"I'm not worried about my Christmas present, Luke."

There was nothing else she wanted from him than what he'd already given her. This whole trip was much more than she'd ever hoped for.

"Why don't you just promise to take more time for yourself after you get back?" she asked. "That would be a great present, because then this wouldn't have all been for nothing."

He eased her back and came to hover over her. The way he always maneuvered her to where he wanted her was just another layer of sexy she hadn't anticipated.

"You can ask me for anything," he told her. "Consider it yours."

Could they try to keep a physical relationship once they returned? Was that even possible? Because at this point, she wasn't sure she could just turn off that switch and act like nothing had happened between them…

But was continuing their sexual liaison something Luke wanted? Was he even thinking that far ahead? She wanted to give him some time to get used to this. She'd had years to accommodate to her feelings, but everything was still so new to him.

"No Christmas present necessary," she reiterated. "There's nothing I need." *But then again...*

Kelly eased her knees up beside his hips to allow him to settle in between her legs. Then she laced her fingers behind his neck. "Or maybe we could come up with something you could give me."

Nodding approvingly, Luke slid his hand up the hem of her cover-up and found her more than ready. She cried out and pushed into his touch.

"I'm sure I can do something for you," he promised.

Making love by the ocean in the dark of the night was a moment she would never forget. Kelly hoped this was just the beginning of their intimate relationship and that her boss would want to keep things going once they returned home.

Thirteen

"I didn't take you for someone afraid of heights."

Luke held onto the edge of the deck and stared across the vast expanse of trees and lines. Nothing like looking like a complete wimp in front of the woman who went to so much trouble to prepare these plans.

"I'm not afraid of heights," he scoffed, trying not to lose his breakfast. "I'm just…getting acclimated, that's all."

"Sir, you do not have to go," the worker assured him. "We have people all the time that back out. It's different once you get up here and see."

"I'm not backing out," he stated.

Damn it, he *wouldn't*. He ran a multi-billion-dollar company and he'd never shied away from a challenge in his life. There was nothing he'd ever turned away from when he wanted it. And he damn well wanted to impress Kelly right now.

"Do you want me to go first?" she asked, placing a gentle hand on his arm.

He glanced to her, finding her absolutely adorable in her protective gear, with worry glimmering in her eyes. She'd do anything for him. She'd proven that over and over again. Now he needed to man up and show her that he wasn't someone who couldn't have a good time.

Unfortunately, his idea of a good time was hitting the weight room or going for long-distance runs. Nice things on solid ground. That was more his style.

Flying never bothered him, but this…this was a whole different level of crazy. Now there was just a thin cable holding him up and he wasn't necessarily a small guy.

"I'll go first," he gritted out, ignoring the churning in his gut. "Let's do it."

He listened once again as the worker went over the basic rules and what to do at the other end. Finally, he stepped to the edge, pushed aside the fear that nearly took him out at the knees and just stepped off.

The second he dropped and started gliding, he squeezed his eyes shut. But then something changed within him. His trepidation gave way to exhilaration and the smooth ride seemed almost *liberating*. Luke opened his eyes to see the treetops below and the bright beautiful ocean in the distance. Before he knew it, he was landing on the other deck and another worker was patting his back on a job well done.

Luke turned in time to see Kelly's big, wide smile as she rushed toward him from the cable. She was absolutely breathtaking like this. And apparently had needed this adrenaline rush just as much as he did.

Something shifted inside him once again. There was something about her that propelled him to take risks, that had him wanting to know even more about what made her smile like she hadn't a care in the world.

"You did it!" she exclaimed. "Did you like it?"

Luke nodded as he was assisted in removing his helmet. "I did. It was pretty awesome."

"I really am sorry I terrified you."

Luke didn't want pity, good grief that was like just adding salt into the wound. He might as well turn in his man card.

"Honestly, I didn't know heights bothered me that much until now," he admitted.

"Do you want to go again?" she asked.

There was a sparkle in her eyes that he couldn't resist. This woman was a risk-taker, which was a hell of a turn-on. He wanted to see that smile more. He wanted her to be happy. And most importantly, he wanted to be the man to ensure that joy never faltered.

This side of Kelly was not one he typically saw in the office and he realized he wanted to keep uncovering those layers to find out her true essence.

He dropped a kiss to her lips. "Let's go."

After several hours of zip-lining and hiking through trails along the mountainside, they headed back to the resort in their Jeep. Kelly loved the freedom of driving with the top down along the ocean road and having Luke by her side made the experience even more special.

"How about a walk along the beach?" she suggested once they were back inside their bungalow.

"Sounds good to me."

She slid her arms around his waist and stared up at him. "I really am sorry you were scared earlier. I just assumed—"

"That I was brave?" he laughed. "Don't tell anyone I nearly passed out looking at treetops."

"Your secret is safe with me," she assured him. "We're all afraid of something."

His brows drew in as he tipped his head, studying her. "You've found my kryptonite. What's yours?"

Kelly's heart clenched. What she *truly* wanted, more than anything was a family of her own one day. And a solid, loving relationship with a man who would put her first. But that man could not be Luke, no matter how much she might want him to be. There was no use in getting her hopes up or even letting her mind go in that direction. She'd been with him for five years and it wasn't like one week of great sex would reprogram this incurable workaholic.

"I think a girl needs to keep some secrets." She smiled and kissed his bearded chin. "Let's get our suits on and go to the beach. Maybe wear that suit you had from the first day."

"That tight thing? It will cut off circulation to the most important parts."

Kelly slid her hand between them and cupped those said parts. "Well, we certainly can't have that. I have plans for us later."

He instantly jerked against her palm. "Later?"

She couldn't help but smile as she eased her hand inside the waistband of his shorts for full-on contact.

"Now is fine, too."

Luke groaned and dropped his head back. This is what she wanted. She wanted him to come undone for her, knowing she'd caused him to release such passion. For now, he was hers, and she planned on taking full advantage...*literally.*

She eased his shorts down to his ankles and dropped to her knees.

"Kelly—"

"Let me," she whispered.

His hand went into her hair as she started to pleasure him. She had never done this to any other man and she only wanted this level of intimacy with Luke.

As she continued to stroke him, his hands tightened, pulling her hair just a bit and she knew he was getting closer to the edge. She increased her speed, hoping she was doing this right. But clearly he was enjoying himself and that's all she really wanted.

When the climax overtook him, he grunted her name over and over and the moment turned her on more than she ever dreamed possible. Who knew pleasuring someone else in such a way would be so arousing?

Kelly waited until he was finished before coming back to her feet and adjusting his shorts back into place. She stared up at him, and he smiled back at her.

"I still owed you a favor," she reminded him. "It's not the waterfall, but I couldn't wait."

He framed her face in his big, strong hands and pulled her within a breath of his face.

"You're going to be the death of me," he murmured. "What am I going to do with you?"

Was it too soon to ask about continuing this physical relationship once they returned? He was still adjusting to this fantasy life they were living. And she knew everything might be entirely different once they were back in Royal.

Would he still be married to his work or would he find a way to make room in his life for her?

She was reminded yet again of growing up with a father who was a workaholic. Kelly and her mother always came in behind board meetings or work trips. Her father loved them in his own way, but he just prioritized his life in the wrong order.

Luke had done that with his fiancée, but they weren't compatible so…what all did that mean? Would he consider putting her first in any manner?

Wanting anything more than a fling was so naive, but there was that sliver inside of her that wondered if anything more would be possible. Kelly shouldn't allow her thoughts to stray, yet there they were. She was human and had waited so long for Luke to see her as more and now…hell. She was in trouble. She knew it, but how did anyone just turn off feelings?

"Hey."

Luke's intense stare and calming word pulled her away from her thoughts.

"Sorry," she told him. "I was daydreaming."

He slid his thumb across her lower lip. "I'd love to hear about your dreams."

Kelly hadn't expected that. She hadn't expected him to want to learn more about her as a person, so maybe he *was* interested in exploring more. With every fiber of her being, she wanted someone to share her hopes and dreams with, someone to confide in, someone she could discuss her day with.

She couldn't help but smile at the idea of going

to work together and coming home and unwinding with a drink cozied up on the couch.

Damn it! Why was she going there again? She couldn't want more with him, she absolutely could not. An intimate relationship was pushing it once they returned. Asking or wanting more was just waiting for a crushed heart.

"Let's go take that walk on the beach," she told him. "Then maybe we can have a relaxing swim in our pool later after dinner."

"During the sunset," he added. "I never thought I'd appreciate a sunset until I spent this time here with you."

He had so much going on with his family and with Wingate Enterprises. What would happen if they got back home and he left all these feelings behind? Would he just go back to business as usual? Would they keep their affair a secret?

There were so many questions swirling around in her mind. Kelly wished she had all the answers, but all she could do was continue to guard her heart and show Luke she wasn't ready for this to end.

"I think we're late for dinner again."

Luke wrapped his arms around Kelly as they sat in the sand. She'd nestled between his legs and leaned back against his chest as they watched the sunset over the ocean. He didn't recall ever feeling this calm or stress-free before. And, while he wasn't sure if this was because of the tranquil atmosphere or Kelly or the amazing sex, part of him never wanted this to end.

The other part knew he had to get back to Royal and help his family pull Wingate back from the brink. There were so many people counting on this company to keep them employed and that was aside from his own family. He wanted to make something grand happen so he could ensure Ava kept her beloved company and didn't have to sell off anything else just to live. She didn't deserve that and Luke was damn well going to be the one to save Wingate.

Yet for the past couple of days, he'd forgotten all about his phone and work emails. He'd forgotten the burden that would be waiting for him upon his return.

All he'd wanted to do was lose himself in Kelly and this place. She'd whisked him off like some dream, knowing exactly what he'd needed to pull him out of the work cycle he'd been drowning in.

He hadn't seen it for himself—or maybe he hadn't wanted to. But Kelly had. She'd been in tune with him from day one. No matter what he'd needed, she'd been there by his side. How had he missed the fact she had personal feelings for him?

Because he'd been utterly consumed with saving the world, at least that's what it felt like most days, and he'd had complete tunnel vision.

That's what had ended his engagement, though

he wasn't sorry that had happened. The feelings he had for Kelly over these past few days far surpassed anything he'd ever felt before.

And that scared the hell out of him.

"You're thinking," she murmured, wrapping her arms around his over her chest. "I can practically hear you."

"Just thinking of work," he admitted.

Kelly tipped her head back and stared up at him. "That's not allowed."

He kissed her forehead. "I know, but I'm just wondering how you could be so aware of what I needed and I couldn't see that you had feelings for me."

"Who said I had feelings? Maybe I just wanted to jump your bones."

Luke laughed. "Because I'm wide awake now and I can see it. You wouldn't have gone to all this trouble for seclusion and you sure as hell wouldn't have been intimate with me if you didn't harbor strong feelings."

She rested her head back against his shoulder and crossed her ankles out in front of her.

"No, I wouldn't have," she admitted. "But I also know this intimacy is all we can have. I won't play second fiddle to anything, not even a career. I just wanted you to see me as more and I wanted to take this chance to make that happen."

Oh, he saw her. He had no idea what to do now with all these emotions raging inside of him. Hearing her say she wouldn't come second to anything made sense, but there was a ping of disappointment that she agreed they couldn't be more. Clearly that's what he had thought, but having the words out in the open seemed so final.

But what about a physical relationship? Who said they had to stop once they returned to Royal?

Only time would tell, and their days here were quickly coming to an end. They would both have to decide what would happen once they returned home and Luke had to find out if there was room in his life for anything other than Wingate.

Fourteen

Kelly let herself back in the bungalow after going to the gift shop once more. She'd seen a new sundress she wanted in the window the other day, but had gotten sidetracked by Luke and hadn't gotten around to buying it. So she'd left him out on the patio drinking by the pool after their lunch and finally purchased it. She couldn't believe they were leaving tomorrow morning. A part of her wanted to stay here forever, but they had to get back and start work again.

Not to mention the Christmas parties coming up, and then rolling into the new year, which would mean more meetings regarding the best ways to increase sales and generate new ideas for the company.

Kelly snuck into her room where she still kept her clothes, but she'd been spending her nights in Luke's bed. She slid into the new strapless white dress that hugged her curves and had a wide slit going from her ankle to mid-thigh.

She made her way to the patio and stepped outside. Luke stood facing the ocean with his back to her, clearly still wet from his time in the pool.

"You like?" she asked, holding her arms out to the side.

He turned around and his mouth dropped. "That's damn sexy."

As much as his compliment warmed her, she couldn't help but notice what he was holding. Kelly's arms dropped to her sides as she took a step toward him.

"How did you get your phone?"

He had the widest smile on his face. "I saw you punch in the code once and I'm glad I did because I just had the best idea and I couldn't wait to text Zeke about it."

"What was that?"

As much as she didn't want work life to interfere with what they had here, they *were* leaving tomorrow. She just wished she could've kept him from this for one more day. She wasn't ready for that other life to creep in on their alone time.

"Why don't we package our resorts to couples?" he suggested. "Instead of trying to appeal to families or corporate events, I think we should look into romantic getaways. Honeymoons, anniversaries, just-because trips. We need to market those to make guests feel like you and I do. Like work doesn't exist or matter and they can escape from their problems."

But work *did* exist and he was proving that. She wanted to take that phone away…she wanted to focus back on them. But Luke had been away from work for four days now and, clearly, he couldn't take it anymore.

"That's great," she told him, forcing a smile. "I'm glad you came up with a solution that will work."

"Do you really think it will?" he asked.

That was one other thing about him. He always valued her opinion and seriously wanted her input on each phase of anything he worked on at Wingate.

"If we can get guests to feel like us, then I think our hotels will skyrocket with bookings. You would have to think of not only the rooms and how that is laid out, but also the staff. You would need the couples to feel like they are one-on-one with a particular staff member. For instance, they need to be on a first name basis and know they can call upon one of our employees for anything at any time."

Her mind started working even though that was the last thing she wanted. But she couldn't help herself. Maybe a little of Luke rubbed off on her.

"Privacy will be the key to any couples' retreat,"

she added. "You want them to feel like they are living in a dream."

Luke stepped forward, set his phone on the patio table and slid his hands around her hips. He glided those talented fingers up into the dip in her waist and higher until he reached the top of her dress where it stopped just at the swell of her breasts.

"Is that what you feel like?" he asked huskily. "Like you're living in a dream?"

Kelly pulled in a deep breath as arousal coursed through her. The man had barely touched her, and she was ready to go up in flames. Would he always affect her this way? Would she always want him with such a fierceness that she couldn't even describe?

"I *am* living a dream," she admitted, closing her eyes to his touch.

Luke peeled the dress down over her chest, leaving her bare to the warm, evening breeze.

"You're so damn sexy, Kel."

He'd never called her by a nickname before and, now that he had, she couldn't help but wonder if they'd reached a deeper level of intimacy.

His thumbs raked over her nipples and she wished he'd tear this dress off of her...who cared that she'd just bought it. Having Luke lose his control and have his way with her would be worth it.

His cell vibrated on the table and she nearly cursed.

"Leave it," she begged.

He hesitated for a split second and she thought for sure he was going to reach for it, but he ended up lifting her into his arms and walking inside.

"I have more important things to tend to," he told her. "Work can wait."

Her heart leapt with joy. She'd never seen him put work on hold for anything and now he was putting it on hold for her…for them. Maybe Luke had changed over the course of this trip.

He carried her into his room and sat her down at the foot of the bed. She'd gotten wet from his trunks and bare skin, but she didn't care. A man who looked like Luke should never be clothed. Kelly could stare at him all day long and never tire of it.

Her hand went to his side, where she saw the tail of the dragon tattoo.

"What's this about?" she asked.

"Strength. After my parents died and Ava took Zeke and me in, I vowed to remain strong no matter what. I vowed that I would take care of my family, my friends and never let anyone fall."

Which was why he was so damn protective of Wingate. She understood his burning need to save the company, but he couldn't keep carrying the weight of the world on his shoulders.

"I never thought a tattoo could be such a turn-on," she murmured, tracing her finger along the point of the tail and back up the other side.

His body trembled beneath her touch and he kept those dark eyes locked onto her.

"What am I going to do with you?"

She smiled. "You keep asking that. When are you going to figure it out for yourself?"

In lieu of an answer, Luke dipped his head and captured one breast. Kelly's head dropped back as she closed her eyes and slid her hands through his hair to hold on.

The way this man could drive her wild with the simplest of touches was amazing. She whispered his name, begging him for more. And that's when his hand found that slit in her dress that stopped just shy of being indecent.

She'd put nothing on beneath when she tried the dress on, always eager to give him easy access.

"I take it you like my new dress," she murmured.

His hand found her core, and Kelly stepped wide to allow his touch to work over her.

"I'd love you out of it even more," he muttered against her skin.

She gripped the material below her breasts and shoved the stretchy dress down her body. Luke only released her for a moment to get the garment out of the way before he was back on her.

"I need you now," he told her, lifting her to toss her onto the bed.

Kelly laughed once again, because the man went

from erotic to playful so fast, she couldn't keep up. Always keeping her on her toes and wanting more.

He climbed onto the bed and rested a hand on each side of her head.

"I want you," he repeated. "Without a barrier."

His words sunk in and that's when she knew he cared for her more than she thought. He wouldn't want to be this intimate if this was just a casual fling.

Kelly eased her legs apart to accommodate his large frame. "I'm clean and protected without anything."

That jaw muscle clenched as his nostrils flared. He was hanging on by a thread. She could read him so easily now.

With this knowledge, Kelly locked her ankles behind his back and urged him closer to where she so desperately wanted him to be.

Once he sank into her, she couldn't help but cry out. Every time they were together she wanted more. She wanted to consume him and never stop loving him, both physically and mentally.

She did love Luke. There was no denying the facts and, quite possibly, she'd loved him for a long time.

But now she could admit it to herself and not be worried or afraid. Because she had a feeling he might be falling, too.

"You're so damn perfect."

Those whispered words falling from his lips only

heightened her arousal. He was everything to her and she wished she could tell him she loved him.

But she had to wait. There was no way she could pour her heart out to him this soon. He might not believe her and she didn't want to scare him off or confuse him. There was too much going on in his life with his family and the company. Adding to his stress would get them nowhere.

His body rocked harder, faster, his lips seemed to travel everywhere. He covered her face, her neck, back down to her chest, where she instinctively arched to his mouth. Her legs tightened even more around his waist and, with all of the pleasure points being hit at the same time, Kelly lost control and fell over the edge.

Luke followed her, ravaging her mouth as he went, and Kelly kissed him back, hoping her passion and love would come through without saying a word. She needed him to know just how special he was to her and just how much she wanted to be with him.

As they lay in his bed in the silence of the aftermath, Kelly wondered how long she could hold out before confessing that she'd fallen in love with her boss.

Fifteen

The flight back proved to be business as usual. Kelly tried not to take offense. They were, after all, away from the resort and the fantasy they'd been living for five days.

Luke sat across from her on his phone sending emails, then talking, then sending more emails. She had her laptop, but it remained closed at her side. The only reason she'd brought it to begin with was to keep up the ruse that they were meeting with an investor.

She wasn't in the mood now, though she knew there would be plenty of emails and work she could get done. Nothing needed her attention until Monday. She planned on taking tomorrow off and trying to transition from exotic island to Royal, Texas.

"This is going to be amazing," Luke exclaimed, setting his phone at his side. "I need you to take some notes."

Kelly pulled up her phone and sighed. Yup, they were definitely back to business as usual.

"We're going to throw a lavish party," he started. "We're going to have it at the Clubhouse and this needs to be bigger and better than anything we've ever done."

"How soon do you want this?" she asked.

"Next weekend."

Kelly stared across the aisle at him. "Luke, you can't possibly plan something of this magnitude in such a short time."

"Oh, I'm not planning it," he corrected. "We are."

She laughed. "You're insane."

"No, I'm optimistic," he told her. "Listen, we need to do this. My mind is back working overtime and you were so right when you said I needed this break. I know exactly how to fix Wingate and we are going to unveil our plan to our family and friends and look to the future with hope. It's Christmas, Kelly. There's so much to celebrate right now."

Having a festive, holiday party and the big reveal of his idea seemed fun and exciting in theory, but how in the hell would they pull this off?

"Do you even know if the Clubhouse is available that day?" she asked.

Luke merely raised a brow and she realized her question was ridiculous. If Luke Holloway wanted something, he was going to get it.

"Ok, so the venue is done." She made a note in her phone. "What about food or music or decorations?"

"I'm putting you on decorations," he stated. "You've used that one place before."

He snapped his fingers as if trying to recall, but Kelly chimed in with the local company and typed in its name.

"Music and food can be done easily," he told her. "The club has people on file and we will use their services."

Kelly made some quick notes to follow up with all of these people tomorrow...clearly she'd be working Sunday instead of waiting until Monday.

"You've thought of everything," she told him with a smile. "What about banners or pamphlets for guests to see what you're envisioning?"

"Yes, that's where I really need you." He stood up from his seat and crossed the narrow space to sit next to her on the sofa. "We need to pull up all of our resorts and do mock-ups of exactly what we plan on adding to each place. We have to list the new amenities specifically designed for the couples."

He started naming off several things and she was

typing as fast as she could. Maybe she should have brought up her laptop.

By the time they touched down in Royal, Luke was ready to go. He'd already made several calls and had set up meetings…for tonight…as in Saturday night.

Kelly wasn't surprised, but she was still disappointed. Although she should have realized that, the second he was back, the old Luke would take over and hit the ground running.

Perhaps that's part of the reason she loved him. The man was diligent, determined, and let nothing stand in the way of his success. He didn't work for the money; he worked to make things right, to help his family get back their tarnished reputation and regain footing with their company.

As they made their way toward their vehicles, Luke put Kelly's suitcase in her trunk. He had his own suitcase and she honestly didn't know if he'd packed any of his tacky resort wear or if he just had his suits inside. He'd worn a pair of navy dress pants and a dark gray dress shirt for the ride home. But she knew exactly what was beneath all of that. There were no fancy clothes that could erase her memory of every mouthwatering muscle he had, because she'd explored each and every one.

"I'm heading to Zeke's to discuss the plans," he told her, shoving his hands in the pockets of his dress pants. "If we can get this in motion quickly, then we could use all of these pre-bookings at the resorts to really pull the company back up."

"That's a solid plan," she agreed. "Just don't rush too much or everything could backfire and then we'd be worse off than we are now."

He shook his head and sighed. "I doubt things could get worse, but I refuse to let that happen."

Kelly felt his angst, knew the turmoil and the worry that flooded him. She'd seen it firsthand over the past several months. His family had been through hell at the hands of someone they trusted and Luke bore all of the weight of the company upon his shoulders. He didn't want to burden others; he wanted to be the one who came up with some magical resolution.

She also knew how much he loved Ava and appreciated all she had done for him after his parents passed. And Kelly understood that, deep down, his gratitude was the driving force behind him wanting to be the white knight who swooped in and saved the day for the woman who basically raised him.

"Come back to my house," he told her.

Kelly was surprised those words came out of his mouth. She hadn't been sure exactly where they'd land once they returned, but she had planned on letting him set the tone and the pace.

"Aren't you going to see your brother?"

Luke nodded and took a step toward her. He

reached for her, curling his hands around her shoulders and pulling her close.

"I am, but I want you at my house when I get back." He dropped a kiss to her lips, then eased back. "I want you by my side through this."

As his assistant or his mistress…or something more? She wanted to ask, but the pain laced with worry in his eyes had her simply nodding in agreement.

"I'll be there."

"You know the code to let yourself in, right?"

Being his assistant for five years had given her access to nearly everything in his life. She'd never been to his house for more than quick drop-offs or pickups for various work things, but she wasn't about to turn down his invitation. This might be their chance to see if they could be more.

"Good luck with Zeke." She stepped back and opened the driver's door. "I'm going to pick up some things at my place and then I'll be at yours."

Luke smiled. "I like the sound of that."

Then he turned and went to his vehicle and Kelly was left wondering exactly what he was thinking as far as they were concerned.

All she knew was Luke had recharged and seemed more hopeful than she'd seen him in a long time. Maybe he needed her emotional support, maybe he wanted more. No matter what, she still had to guard her heart. Even though she'd fallen for him, she still realized Luke wasn't going to put aside his work to make her first in his life. No matter how much she wanted a family and a husband, Luke could not fill that role. All she could do was enjoy their time together until it came to an inevitable end.

"It's genius."

Luke released a sigh of relief and sank back into the leather sofa in his brother's living room. Zeke sat across from him on the other sofa with his wife, Reagan, by his side.

His brother and sister-in-law had found love in the most unconventional of ways. A fake relationship for a front fell apart, but the two had married in Vegas anyway…and then fell in love. A little backward, but everything worked out in the end for Zeke and Reagan. Luke couldn't imagine them apart. They were so perfect for each other and complemented one another in every way.

Reagan slid her hand over Zeke's thigh and offered a sweet smile. "Luke, you have been so stressed lately. It's nice to see you relaxed. Wherever you went on a trip sure did wonders for your smile."

Luke wasn't about to admit anything or why he was smiling so much. Kelly had pulled something from him he hadn't even known was so hidden and buried. After months of working so damn hard, staying up countless nights, worrying if he'd ever come up with the answer, Luke finally had a solution, and he only had her to thank.

"Kelly played a huge part in coming up with this plan," he admitted. "She's brilliant."

"You're a lucky man to have such an amazing right-hand-woman," Reagan stated.

Assistant seemed so odd a term now. A week ago Kelly was his assistant and now, well, she was his assistant, lover, and he wasn't sure what else to label her, because he was still trying to figure all of this out himself.

Between Wingate and his unexpected feelings for Kelly, Luke really had no idea which way to direct his attention right now. There was so much going on at once, tearing him from one side of his heart to the other.

He cared for Kelly, there was no denying that. Making any type of label beyond that was naive and foolish. Just because his brother had found the love of his life didn't mean that was in the cards for Luke. He had much too much on his plate right now to feed a relationship. Look at that past engagement? That had been a disaster.

"Kelly *is* amazing," he agreed. "She's working right now on getting the arrangements all set up for the party at the Clubhouse this Saturday."

"So I take it you're not angry with me for deceiving you with this getaway?" Zeke asked.

Angry? How could he be angry? That had been

one of the best weeks of his life. But he didn't like that Zeke paid for everything and he would be rectifying that soon. He just didn't want to get into a financial argument right now.

"You look like a different guy," his brother added. "You don't have those frown lines and you don't look so pissed off at the world. Maybe we should incorporate forced vacations quarterly to keep everyone at the top of their game."

Another trip with Kelly? He sure as hell wouldn't turn that down.

"I hate admitting you were right," Luke stated. "But we need to push forward and focus on this party this weekend."

Zeke chuckled. "You don't waste any time, brother."

"We don't have the time to waste. We need these pre-sales. That money will help launch us into the next phase."

"This is big," Zeke agreed, sliding his hand over Reagan's. "I knew you'd stop at nothing to come up with some miracle way to preserve the company."

Pride swelled within him. Luke hoped like hell this plan worked and would help protect the jobs of their two hundred workers. This next plan wasn't just about saving his own ass, but looking out for those who would have to seek employment elsewhere if something happened to Wingate.

"It's not going to solve everything," Luke replied.

"But, it's a solid start that will have our shareholders and investors believing in us again. This will definitely boost everyone's moral."

"I think it sounds wonderful." Reagan beamed as she patted Zeke's leg. "You and Kelly have really outdone yourselves with this plan."

Luke knew his brilliant assistant was the backbone of his operation. He literally couldn't do his job to the best of his ability with anyone else by his side. Never in his life had he thought he'd find someone so compatible in the boardroom and the bedroom.

So what the hell did that all mean?

"Beyond the amenities—" Luke went on, forcing himself to stay focused on work "—we should add in upgraded packages for when someone really wants to impress or go all out. We can offer up private jet transportation and a car once they reach their destination. Our guests shouldn't have to worry about one thing once they book with Wingate."

Reagan's smile widened. "This will be a total sell-out," she announced.

"I couldn't do any of this without Kelly."

Zeke tipped his head and drew his brows in. "Did something happen on this trip?"

"Yeah, we came up with a genius plan."

"Beyond that," his brother clarified. "Is there something more going on?"

Luke had no idea how Zeke had honed in on that,

other than the fact they were brothers and shared a very close bond.

"Zeke, she's my assistant."

His brother continued to study him with that dark gaze that resembled his own.

"Nice dodge of the question," he said. "Something did happen. I can tell. You know, it's ok to admit anything. I know you feel the weight of the company on your shoulders, but you're not alone in this. Kelly is a great woman and she'd be good for you."

There was absolutely no way in hell Luke would ever admit anything to his brother...not this early in their relationship.

Wait. *Relationship?*

Yeah, he supposed it could have that label, but just because they were physical and he'd asked her to stay at his house didn't mean he was ready by any means to settle down.

Luke shrugged. "All that happened was Kelly finally got me to see that I needed to recharge because I was being too hard on myself and that wasn't doing anyone any good. The getaway really helped me see things so much clearer."

All of that was the truth, Luke just opted to omit the R-rated version of the trip. Everything going on between Kelly and him had to remain confidential. Letting anyone else inside their personal bubble wasn't an option...not even his brother.

"I'm not so sure that's all there is to tell," Zeke added.

Reagan smacked his leg. "Would you leave the guy alone? He's come up with a brilliant plan to save Wingate and make the company profitable again. If something is going on in his personal life with his assistant, that's his business."

Luke could jump across the coffee table between them and kiss his sister-in-law. She had a way of keeping Ezekiel in line. Zeke never backed down to anyone, but he would do literally anything his wife told him to do and he'd do it with a smile on his face.

Luke wasn't about to say anything more. He didn't want to lie to his brother and he sure as hell didn't want to discuss Kelly.

A part of him was thrilled knowing she'd be back at his home waiting for him. He wondered if she was currently exploring his house, his bedroom. Maybe she'd be waiting in the bed or the hot tub on his balcony off his master suite.

Luke came to his feet, more than ready to get home and start working on this party in a relaxed atmosphere with Kelly.

His brother and Reagan also stood and started toward the foyer.

"I'll go ahead and send some texts out about the party," Reagan told him. "I'll be sure to really talk it up as one not to be missed. Christmas is a magical time and I really think the timing couldn't be better for you guys to unveil this endeavor."

"I hope so," Luke replied. "I'll have some banners printed up with marketing and copy you on the email with the design."

"Sounds good," Zeke said with a nod of approval. "I'll start getting the word out to the TCC members, as well."

By the time Luke left and was headed home, he finally felt a sense of accomplishment. He hadn't had this feeling in so long and he absolutely owed everything to Kelly. Before their trip to Hawaii, he'd worked for hours on end, never finding anything resembling a solution that would help Wingate get that extra leg up they needed. But now everything was falling into place.

Luke stifled a yawn as he maneuvered the roads that took him home. It had been a hell of a week in the very best way and he couldn't wait to lie in his own bed tonight. Yet, much as he wanted her right beside him, a part of him wondered if asking Kelly to stay had been a mistake. He sure as hell didn't want to give her the wrong impression or to make her believe they could be more. Luke's hands clenched around the steering wheel as more self-doubts began to creep in. He knew Kelly well enough to know she would get attached and he didn't want to be the one to break her heart.

Sixteen

"Something smells good."

Kelly turned toward the wide, arched opening of Luke's kitchen and smiled as he stepped through.

"I made dinner," she stated, spreading her hands open to the display on the island. "I hope you don't mind. I rummaged through your cabinets to find something. I figured you'd be hungry when you got home."

Nerves swirled her belly as he came on into the kitchen and stood on the other side of the island. Being in his house was so much different than the neutral ground they were in in Oahu. She'd felt so strange walking through his house when she'd first gotten here. For one thing, the place was enormous. She'd peeked in each of the six bedrooms and deduced his was the one done in all navy and rich woods and the entire room had his masculine essence.

Everything in this place reminded her of him. The classy decor, the strong beams accenting the ceiling, the commanding two-story stone fireplace in the living room. It was all quintessential Luke and she loved getting another insight to his personal life.

Zeke and Luke had been living together, but Zeke had moved in with Reagan once they married. Kelly could easily see two bachelors living here in this vast domain.

She'd spotted a photo of Luke's parents on his dresser, and a piece of her heart tumbled for him. She knew that ache of not having parents in your life. At least he had his brother and aunt. He had some family left and she was glad he still had a strong bond with those in his life.

Kelly longed for such a bond but, more than that, she longed for a life partner. She longed for a family of her own and a man who loved her. She saw how her mother had missed out on so much and Kelly knew she would never live that way.

"I didn't mean to be gone so long," he told her. "Zeke and I got to talking, and I just wanted to make sure I filled him in on every detail."

"What did he think?" she asked. "Was Reagan there, too?"

Luke nodded. "They both thought it was brilliant. Reagan is sending out some texts and phone calls to some of her friends and Zeke is talking to the members of the club."

"It's going to be a busy week getting everything ready," she told him. "I hope I can pull all of this off to your satisfaction."

Luke circled the island and came to stand directly in front of her. Taking her hands, he looked directly into her eyes.

"You will pull it off," he assured her. "There's not a doubt in my mind that this will be the greatest party and re-launch ever. You're a mastermind when it comes to organizing and bossing people around."

Kelly couldn't help but laugh and shake her head. "I'm not bossy."

"You did a hell of a job bossing me in Oahu," he reminded her, then placed a quick, sweet kiss on the tip of her nose. "I need to grab a shower before I eat. I'm still straight off the plane and I want to change."

"No problem. I'll just fix up a plate and get us some wine."

He stared at her for a moment and she thought he was going to say something, but he ended up just releasing her hands.

"Give me ten minutes," he told her before he left the room and headed toward the stairs.

Kelly hoped he didn't mind coming home to her in the kitchen like she belonged here. She'd gotten fidgety waiting on him and then her stomach had started growling. Next thing she'd known she was boiling pasta and making marinara sauce.

Searching through the cabinets once again, she found plates and utensils. It took a bit to find the wine opener, but then she realized he had an electric one on the counter above the wine fridge.

When he still hadn't come down, she wondered if he'd gotten busy with emails or phone calls. She waited nearly twenty minutes before heading upstairs to check on him.

The minute she rounded the corner of his bedroom, she stopped short. There he was wearing only a towel around his waist, face down on his bed… fast asleep.

A twinge of disappointment coursed through her. So much for a romantic evening and picking up where they'd left off at the resort.

Kelly snuck away and went back downstairs. After eating a quick dinner, she cleaned up the kitchen and put the leftovers away. She'd already showered and changed at her place before she came here and now she needed to unwind. Her mind was racing and her thoughts too revved up to go to sleep.

With her laptop and phone, she decided to go to the back enclosed patio that overlooked the pond.

The cozy oversize chaise in the corner called her name the moment she'd seen it earlier.

She settled in and started working on emails, spreadsheets, decor ideas, and everything that would be involved in throwing a last minute, lavish party. Her work was definitely cut out for her, but she'd never failed Luke before, and she certainly didn't intend to start now. Their professional relationship was stronger than ever, but she had no clue about their romantic future. She had a sinking feeling someone was going to get hurt…and that someone would likely be her.

"As you can see here, there would be specialty suites in an entirely different area of our resorts."

Luke pointed to the mock-up slide he'd put up on the screen in the boardroom. Kelly sat at the opposite end of the table and tried to gauge the faces of everyone in attendance.

Ava seemed completely enthralled at the ideas Luke presented. She'd eased forward in her seat, with her brows raised, and it was clear her nephew had her undivided attention.

Zeke seemed relaxed, as usual, as he sat back in his leather chair. The other board members were all staring up at the screen and, every now and then, Luke would glance her way and the butterflies would start fluttering all over again.

She'd spent the past two nights at his house, but

this morning he'd been up and gone before she even woke. Since Saturday night, they had shared a bed, but nothing more than a few sultry kisses had been exchanged. He was all in work-mode and ready to get this morning meeting to the members of the board.

He'd been so restless last night. At one point she'd just rested her hand on his back and he'd calmed down. She knew he was nervous, but she also knew this whole plan was so splendid, there would be no way it would fail.

She didn't want to bring up the proverbial elephant: their relationship. Once this party was over and they were riding the high of moving forward, she would talk to him. He deserved to know how she felt and give him the chance to tell her how he felt.

They were so connected on the island, and they weren't necessarily disconnected here, but they also weren't as open and talkative. Right now it was just all work. She wanted more…she shouldn't, but she did.

"We can still appeal to the corporate travelers," Luke went on, pulling her focus back to the meeting. "But that will no longer be our target audience. We will transform seventy percent of all resort rooms to accommodate couples for special, tranquil retreats. And we will offer a diverse range of packages for people on a budget all the way up to people who don't care how much they have to spend for their significant other."

Luke pivoted from the screen and tapped on his laptop, then turned back to the new slide.

"This would be the projected budget," he added. "And if you look on the next slide, you will see the projections of income if we have eighty percent booked by spring."

Kelly watched him in action, never more proud of the position he was in and the stand he was taking to protect his family, his company and the employees who depended on Wingate.

"This is a risk," Ava finally said when Luke was finished.

Luke nodded in agreement, his eyes meeting Kelly's briefly. She gave him a reassuring nod and he focused his attention back to his aunt.

"There's going to be a risk in any decision we make moving forward," he agreed. "This is the best-case scenario. Honeymooners, couples celebrating anniversaries, someone trying to get back in a partner's good graces, or a suitor pulling out all the stops to win someone's love…these are all everyday people who need a nice, reputable resort. Wingate can and will provide those services and be the greatest name when people go to book their getaways."

"Reagan's ready to book the first platinum package," Zeke chimed in. "I reminded her we already have a private jet at our disposal."

Ava tapped her short nails on the glossy table and Kelly couldn't stop staring, waiting for her final reaction. Although she knew the family matriarch wouldn't have the ultimate say on the matter, especially since the party and roll-out were already in place. This board meeting was more of a formality and a heads-up so everyone would be on the same page and able to answer any questions at the event.

"I trust you on this," Ava told Luke and Zeke. "I know you boys wouldn't steer this company in the wrong direction. You clearly believe this is the way to go and I am behind you a hundred percent."

Luke smiled, and Kelly could see the relief cross his face. He wanted Ava's approval. They'd been through so much together since his parents' passing. Not only had they been through heartache personally, they had also endured it professionally.

And with Keith being exposed as the criminal bastard he was, that had been another hard blow to all of them. He'd been a trusted figure in their lives. Now he was behind bars awaiting a trial. Kelly didn't even know how difficult that day would be when several of them had to testify…namely Ava and Luke.

"We have marketing working on the designs and various information for the guests this weekend," Luke went on. "Kelly has already contacted their caterer and set up the music. She's got the decor sorted out, as well."

"We'll be working around the Christmas decor the Clubhouse already has in place, but it will have a flare for romantic getaways, as well," she told everyone.

Luke caught her eye again, and she smiled. Then he went on to discuss the party in more detail and the way the evening would play out and the roles each of them would have.

Kelly continued to add to her notes. Luke had already gone over everything with her before they came in, but as he spoke, more ideas popped into her head and she wanted to type them in before she forgot. They needed to send out a company-wide memo in addition to an invitation to the party with a message to bring as many guests as possible. This needed to be a grand event to celebrate Wingate's big comeback.

As the meeting came to an end and everyone filed out the door, Kelly saw Zeke go to the head of the conference table and mutter something to his brother. Luke glanced up to her and she stilled.

"Could you excuse us?" Luke asked.

Kelly nodded and gathered her laptop and left the room, pulling the door closed behind her. She didn't know what the brothers needed to discuss, but she had a sinking feeling this wasn't about work and had everything to do with her.

"What the hell are you doing?" Zeke demanded.

Luke stared at his brother. "About what?"

"Don't act like you don't know what I'm talking about."

Rubbing his coarse beard, Luke shook his head. "I don't know. I thought the meeting went really well."

Zeke stepped closer. "You mean while you were shooting smiles and heart eyes at your assistant at the other end of the table? I asked what happened in Oahu and you denied everything."

Luke pulled in a deep breath. Had other people noticed? Had Ava or the few other members around the table? Hopefully they'd been too focused on the presentation to catch anything he had been unaware he was giving off.

"Do you want to tell me what's going on with Kelly?" Zeke asked. "And don't tell me she's just your assistant. I know that trip changed both of you."

"Fine. She's more. Is that what you want to hear?"

Zeke stared for another minute before taking a step back and cursing beneath his breath.

"What in the world are you thinking?" he demanded. "We're in crisis-mode. That wasn't my intention when I sent you on that trip."

"What I do in my spare time is none of your damn business." Luke willed himself to have patience here, because his brother didn't know the details. "Kelly and I have nothing to do with you."

Zeke nodded. "When it starts interfering with meetings, it sure as hell does."

His brother continued to glower at him, obviously waiting on more of an explanation.

"Kelly and I got closer on the trip," Luke added. "Details aren't necessary, but that's how we came up with this idea for Wingate."

Silence surrounded them and Luke hated that he felt like he had to justify his actions when none of this was Zeke's concern.

"Nobody is aware and I want things to stay that way," Luke explained. "Kelly wasn't just a fling and she's not fodder for office gossip."

Zeke's brows drew in as he jerked slightly in obvious surprise. "You care for her."

This was sure as hell not a conversation Luke had time for, nor did he want to get into with his brother at the office. There were too many other things to be doing, and Luke hadn't even sorted out his emotions yet. If he had serious feelings, then Kelly was the first person who needed to know.

"Your silence speaks for itself," Zeke stated.

"My silence is because I'm ignoring you. Nothing is said to Kelly or anyone else."

Zeke's face split into a wide grin. "Hey, if you want to keep your love life a secret, that's fine. But it will come out sooner or later."

Luke absolutely refused to answer. He could only handle so much at one time and he was juggling too many balls. If he dropped any, there would be another crisis.

He couldn't let Wingate down and he couldn't let Kelly down, either. He cared too much for the both of them and that scared the hell out of him.

Seventeen

Kelly hung her dress back in the walk-in closet and zipped the garment bag before closing the closet doors. She couldn't believe she had time to find a dress and one that fit perfectly without alterations.

She wanted to look her best for the party and for Luke. Every detail had been worked out and the buzz around Royal was spreading like wildfire, with everyone wondering what the announcement could be from Wingate.

Luke had worked late every night this week, falling into bed almost immediately after he'd gotten in. They'd barely talked, except at work, while finishing up the final touches of the party. But he had so much more to do, because the resorts were all being informed of the upgrades and the changes. He'd been busy, in contact with all of those managers and having conference calls.

He'd stolen a few kisses and ass-grabs here and there, but nothing more. The real world really did hit them hard now that they were back, but there was so much to be done to move into this next phase.

She still felt a little strange being at his house, but since he'd asked her to stay, he'd never mentioned her leaving and she'd fallen into a pattern.

She'd been here nearly a week and they hadn't made love one time. Had she just become an afterthought for him? Had their getaway been just a fling? Why had he asked her to stay to begin with if he didn't want to keep up what they'd had?

Once the party was over tomorrow, she would talk to him about where they stood. She understood his work was important to him, but now that her heart was involved, she didn't want to come second place if he was having feelings for her.

But she had to finesse this carefully. Because on one hand, she didn't want to come across as his needy ex. Kelly truly valued his commitment to his job. But on the other hand, if they were going to try at any type of relationship, she needed to know she was an important part of his life as more than his assistant.

A gnawing pit in her stomach opened up at the

realization that maybe Luke didn't want more. She knew he'd always been career-oriented. That part of his life was actually appealing to her, but he'd never claimed to want a serious relationship. He'd never claimed to want a family or a wife.

Kelly cursed herself for being naive, for letting their trip clog her mind with romantic notions about the two of them that might never be fulfilled. She had to talk to him, openly and honestly, and she had to stop trying to dance around the subject.

Luke needed to know she'd fallen in love with him. He deserved to have all of the information so then he could decide where he stood and what he wanted from this relationship.

She didn't expect him home until late tonight, either. She knew he was at the office with Zeke working on the steps to take to make this transition with the resorts as flawless as possible.

Kelly had spent the evening at the TCC clubhouse decorating and making sure everything was absolutely perfect. She planned on being there tomorrow afternoon, as well. Reagan had offered to meet her and work on the final touches and helping the caterers get everything set out exactly where she wanted the dishes to go for easy flow.

Kelly couldn't help but have that rush of excitement over this party. She felt sexy in her dress and she couldn't wait to show Luke. Maybe tomorrow, after she told him she loved him, they could reconnect and pick up from where they'd left off in Hawaii.

She had hope. The way he looked at her, and the way he appreciated her, gave her that spark of encouragement. She wasn't one to be clingy or beg, though. If Luke didn't have the same feelings or want to work on something more solid than a work relationship or a quick fling, then she would have to move on. Just because she felt so strongly, didn't mean that he did. Her feelings had nurtured and grown over the years and Luke had just seen her as little more than his right-hand-woman less than two weeks ago.

Kelly tried to put her nerves to rest and decided to give herself a home manicure and pedi. She wanted to look her best for the re-launch party, and she just needed a little self-care time.

Tomorrow was going to be memorable in both her personal and professional life. She only hoped everything went the way she'd hoped and planned… otherwise, her heart was going to be shattered. If he didn't want more, they would have to part ways in all aspects and that meant she'd have to find a new employer. She had no Plan B, but while she was confident she could recover from her job, she wasn't so sure she'd bounce back from losing Luke.

"Wow. You look hot."

Kelly laughed and did a slow turn in her emerald green strapless ball gown. Reagan let out a slow whistle and a clap.

"There won't be a single man here with his eyes in his head," Reagan laughed. "And maybe some women, too. Damn, that dress is *amazing*."

Kelly loved it from the moment she'd seen it online. She'd paid for overnight shipping and prayed it would fit. The deep V in the front was nearly indecent, but the flare of the skirt gave it a softer touch. It was the best of both worlds, being classy and sultry at the same time. And the emerald green both set off her red hair and celebrated Christmas. She loved this dress so much, she might never take it off. Cleaning house and doing laundry was about to get a face-lift from her usual sweats and tees.

"I'm not looking for the guests to check out this dress," Kelly stated. "I'd rather they look ahead to book a suite."

Reagan slid her hands in the pockets of her full red shirt and smiled. "Honey, they will flock to those rooms and be sure to tell all their friends they were the first to book at the newest, poshest resorts. And then those friends will get jealous and the trickle down effect will begin."

Kelly sighed. "I hope you're right. I'm so nervous."

"No need to be nervous." Reagan leaned in so the workers setting up the tables wouldn't overhear. "Unless you're nervous how a certain someone is going to react when he sees you in that dress."

Kelly's unease grew even more and she wondered how much Reagan knew.

"Don't worry," the other woman stated with a soft smile. "I don't officially know anything, but I saw the way Luke talked about you the other day, and I see it in your eyes now."

How had Luke talked about her, and what was she giving away right now? Did others know? Was there gossip flooding the office that she didn't know about?

"I can't do this right now," Kelly murmured.

Reagan reached for her hand and gave a gentle squeeze. "I'm so sorry. I didn't mean to freak you out. Listen, believe me when I say I know how it feels to keep a secret about someone you love."

Kelly closed her eyes. "I'm still processing all of this."

"Does he know you love him?"

Kelly shook her head and focused back on her friend. "Please don't say a word to Ezekiel," she begged.

"Of course not." Reagan reached now for both her hands and laughed. "Sometimes girls just need to have their own pact of secrecy."

Relief filled Kelly. She didn't have many girl-friends and due to her long work hours she didn't get out much to socialize. Reagan being close to Zeke just put her in close proximity to Kelly and she found the woman to be absolutely a joy and a treasure. Zeke had really lucked out.

"Thank you," Kelly said, returning the smile. "I'm sorry, I didn't tell you how amazing you look tonight."

"Red is Zeke's favorite color," she stated with a naughty grin. "Sometimes we just have to remind our men what they're dealing with."

Our men. Kelly wasn't sure how true that statement was, but she did like the sound of it. It reminded her of the conversation she wanted to have with Luke later. But, for now, nothing else mattered but this party and the success of Wingate's relaunch. They needed this big push to get off on the right foot for the first of the year.

Over the next hour, Kelly and Reagan worked on making sure the centerpieces were perfect, leaving pamphlets at each place setting. They also displayed information about the new amenities/travel packages in oversize frames and set it out on the informational table where two employees from Wingate would be stationed all night to answer questions and start the booking process.

She couldn't wait for Luke, Ava, and Zeke to see what all had been done to get this new plan off the ground. The idea had come on so quick, Kelly only hoped they weren't missing anything.

"Is there anything else that we need to do before the guests arrive?"

Kelly turned to Reagan and shook her head. "I think we did it. I seriously appreciate all your help."

Reagan moved toward the bar and motioned for the bartender to come over. "I'd say we deserve a celebratory glass of wine before everyone gets here."

"I like how you think," Kelly laughed. "But I might need the bottle to get through this night."

"We've got the time." Reagan smiled and lifted her glass in a mock cheer. "This is going to be a night to remember."

Kelly took a sip of her pinot and welcomed the tart taste. This would indeed be a night to remember.

Eighteen

Luke stepped into the Texas Cattleman's Club lodge and was blown away by the space and everything Kelly had accomplished in such a short time.

He tried to take in everything all at once as he adjusted his Stetson. There were easels propped up all around the ballroom with large, colorful posters exhibiting the new suites designed for romance, the prospected spa rooms, and the showcase also unveiled how the changes would look in the various locations by spring/summer.

His savvy assistant had managed to display everything in rich colors of gold and white, matching the Christmas decor the lodge already had in place.

There were twinkling lights draped like a canopy of stars from the peaked, wood ceilings. Tall Christmas trees adorned with gold accents and glittering ornaments flanked the entrance to the ballroom. And the tables had centerpieces that looked like something straight from the pages of a magazine.

This level of grandeur surpassed his every expectation, and he vowed to give Kelly a raise. Without her, the idea wouldn't have been born and this party would not have met the high standard people had come to expect from the Wingates.

The caterers were setting up the tiered stands with food at each end of the ballroom. The music had started over in the corner and there was a space for dancing. The lodge doors in the back were open to let the crisp air in and allow members to mill about inside and out. Even though it was December, this was still Texas and the evenings weren't too chilly.

Luke scanned the room once again, looking for Kelly. He hadn't seen her before she'd left. He'd gotten up and gone for a run, then he'd gone to see Ava, and by the time he got home, she'd been gone. He knew she and Reagan were working here for the past couple of hours, so he hadn't wanted to bother her. The party was due to start in thirty minutes and he wanted to steal her away for a moment before they were flooded with nearly all of Royal.

He saw a flash of red, but that was Reagan on the other side of the room. His sister-in-law was definitely a knockout, but Luke only had eyes for one woman.

Luke crossed the wood floor. "Reagan," he called as he approached her. He grabbed her hands and kissed her cheek. "You look beautiful as always."

"You don't look so bad yourself," she murmured, offering her signature smile. "If you're looking for Kelly, she's in the back office. She was touching up her hair."

The back office sounded perfect for that alone time he wanted to have with her. Even five minutes of complete privacy would be great. He'd been so busy this week and, when he'd gotten home, he'd always had every intention of stripping her and making love.

Love? That wasn't the term he should be using… not quite yet. But he did feel much more for her now than when they were in Oahu. Her loyalty, her compassion, her drive all matched his, and the more time he spent with her, even though they were back in reality, the more he realized he liked having her in his home. Knowing she was there waiting for him had him more eager to be home than he ever had been. Unfortunately, the timing of this project didn't allow him all that he craved.

The back office door was cracked and he eased it open, glanced in, and nearly gasped at the beauty before him.

She stood at the decorative old floor mirror

propped against the wall in the corner. Her hands were in her hair. which was draped over one shoulder. She wore a shade of green that did amazing things to her skin, her hair, and her eyes.

Kelly caught his gaze in the reflection and her hands instantly stilled. She spun around and that's when he caught the full view of this dress that would surely bring him to his knees.

Man, he missed their intimacy and he missed when they could just be together without all of these outside complications.

"Kel." He closed the door at his back, unable to take his eyes off of her. "You look… Damn, you look sexy and gorgeous and I don't even know what all else."

She laughed and started toward him. With that full skirt, she seemed to be floating like an angel, but that deep V in the front proved she had a little side of vixen thrown into the mix.

"I was hoping you'd love this," she told him. She reached for his black tie and straightened it, then flattened her hands on his chest. "You look incredible, too."

He could barely speak. Kelly had always been a stunning woman and now that he'd had her in his bed, he knew she was absolutely, utterly perfect.

"Speechless?" she asked, tapping his lips. "That's fine. I plan on doing a good bit of talking later."

Luke swallowed. "I wasn't thinking about talking

at all once I got you home," he assured her, reaching for that dip in her waist just above the skirt. "I owe you so much more after falling asleep on you all week."

Kelly smiled, her red lips practically begging him to mess them up. "I know you've been working hard. It's ok. But we do need to talk."

There was no man alive who wanted to hear those words come out of the mouth of a woman. They never led to anything good.

"That sounds serious," he told her.

She framed his face with her hands and stared back at him with those expressive green eyes. "Nothing to worry about," she promised. "I just have some things I want to tell you."

Luke cringed. "You're pregnant."

"No," she laughed. "Though I do want kids someday. Nice to know where you stand on the topic."

He shook his head as all the thoughts of what she'd want to discuss kept swirling around. "Sorry. I didn't mean to seem paranoid, but well, that would be terrifying right now."

Luke slid his hands along her hips and tugged her closer until her body aligned with his. He captured her lips, needing to feel her, to taste her. He couldn't wait to get her home and peel her out of this dress.

He eased back and stared down into those expressive eyes so full of passion, then she smiled.

"I like my lipstick on you." She slid her thumb

over his lips to clean the mess. "Later, you can mess up the rest of it."

Oh, he loved the sound of that, but he still was itching to know what she wanted to talk to him about. Unfortunately, that would have to wait, because guests were going to be arriving soon and he needed to be out front and center the entire night.

"You did an amazing job out there," he said, taking her hand and leading her toward the door. "In case I haven't said it this week, thank you. It's not much, but I really wouldn't have been able to do this without you."

She tipped her head and the rest of her red curls fell down over her shoulder. "I'm glad I could be the one to help you. This is going to be an extraordinary ride and I want to be on this journey."

Which is exactly where he wanted her.

Later, he would tell her he wanted more. He still wasn't sure exactly what that looked like, but he wanted her to move in with him so they could see where things went.

Luke led Kelly back out to the ballroom, but made sure he wasn't holding her hand or even touching her. He wanted to stop hiding this and just be himself in public with her. He wanted to wrap his arm around her waist and not give a damn what people thought.

Yes, she was his assistant, but there was much more to their relationship. If people wanted to gossip about that, then that was their problem. All he cared about was getting more from Kelly, more from what they had started and seeing where they could go.

Kelly couldn't believe the turnout. She couldn't stop smiling and, every time she glanced around the crowded ballroom, she only saw people having a great time. She had answered questions about the new turn in the Wingate resorts and had even directed many people to the informational area in the back.

Luke and Zeke were milling about and she'd seen them pass by every now and then as they also were busy talking with guests.

The party was most definitely a success.

"I'd say everyone is having a good time."

Kelly turned to see Sutton Wingate, the CFO, nursing a drink and glancing around the room as he came to stand beside her.

"They are," she agreed. "I think this new phase of Wingate is really going to be something huge."

"Luke is taking a chance, but I agree there has to be a big risk for a big payoff."

Sutton's fiancée Lauren came from the bar with a glass of wine in hand and a smile on her face. She looked absolutely stunning in her floor-length gold dress.

"Kelly, you look gorgeous," Lauren stated. "I love that green on you."

"Thanks. I love that gold, too."

Sutton slid an arm around Lauren and a sliver of jealousy slid through Kelly. She wanted to know where she and Luke stood and if they were working toward something. And most of all, she wanted to come out in the open. Stolen kisses and staying at his house, but driving separately to work, wasn't any type of relationship she wanted to have.

"I'm about ready to book one of these getaways myself," Lauren said. "I love my life here, but being pampered with Sutton for a week doesn't sound bad at all."

Kelly gestured toward the back wall. "You can sign up right back there," she joked.

"What's everyone congregating over here for?" Sebastian asked. "Are we having a staff meeting?"

Sutton shook his head at his twin. "Just chatting. The party is already a success. I'm anxious to see the numbers shoot up over the next few weeks with these pre-bookings."

"Always a numbers man," Sebastian joked. "Just relax for the night and let the plan do its work. Everyone is loving the idea of a couple's getaway."

"That's because everyone is getting married or engaged lately," Lauren chimed in with a smile.

Sebastian shook his head. "Not everybody. Right, Kelly?"

She couldn't help but smile at the CEO, who obviously wanted nothing to do with commitment, but he didn't know that's exactly what she wanted from Luke.

"Marriage isn't for everybody," she stated with a shrug. "If you all will excuse me, I need to refill my glass and chat with some guests."

Kelly eased away from the group and nodded her greeting to people she passed by as she moved her way through the crowd. The ballroom was absolutely packed. She was almost positive all of Royal had turned out to see what exactly Wingate was planning next.

She noticed living here that people with money wanted to spend it. They not only strove to have the newest and the nicest things, but they also wanted bragging rights and first dibs on social media status. Fine by her, because that would only give a burst of sales that would create a snowball effect that would generate more money than Wingate had seen since their funds had been pilfered by a trusted source.

Kelly turned and bumped into Gracie Diaz.

"Oh, Gracie," Kelly exclaimed. "I'm so sorry."

Gracie had her hand up to prevent more of a collision and held tightly to a glass of water in her other hand. She looked a little pale, but still gorgeous as always with her long, dark hair and striking brown eyes.

"Are you alright?" Kelly asked.

"Yes, yes. I'm fine." She attempted a smile, but Kelly didn't think Gracie was quite feeling it. "I was just feeling a little tired. I was going to go find a quiet place to sit."

Concerned, Kelly reached for her friend. Gracie scored a winning lottery ticket that had completely changed her life. She was now a multimillionaire and searching for something else to do with her life.

"I was in the back room earlier getting ready," Kelly stated. "I know it's empty if you'd like to go back and close the door. Can I get you something? Do you need to eat or can I get you more water?"

Gracie shook her head. "I just need to sit. I'll be fine, really. Go back to the party."

Kelly hesitated, but the young woman moved away and headed toward the hallway. Kelly wondered what was wrong, but she didn't want to pry. Everyone around here had something they wanted to keep to themselves and Kelly was no different.

Her eyes scanned the room and locked on Luke. He stared across with a hunger in his eyes she'd hadn't seen since Oahu, and her entire body tingled. There might as well be nobody else in the room with the way he was gazing at her.

Beyond the hunger, she saw a desire and a promise staring back. Tonight. She couldn't wait until they were done here and back at Luke's house where they could be alone and she could finally tell him she loved him.

Nineteen

"Your forgiveness means everything," Ava stated as they hovered in the corner of the ballroom at the party.

Luke glanced to Zeke. They'd all had a difficult time after Keith's actions had come to the surface for all to see. Ava obviously didn't know he had been stealing from the Wingates, but Luke and Zeke didn't want a repeat of the past. It was imperative that Sutton keep a tight rein on the numbers of the company and make sure nothing like that ever happened again.

Every division of the company had been impacted and hit hard. So many families had been affected by Keith's embezzlement scheme. The reputation of the company had been tarnished as well and every piece of the company struggled to find footing once again. It was going to happen, but they all knew this would take time and take several steps. Unfortunately, there wasn't just one blanket fix for all.

Justice was served though and Keith would be spending the next fifteen years behind bars where he couldn't hurt anyone again.

"We're only looking forward now," Luke told her. "This next phase is a whole new chapter for everyone."

"I know this isn't the time, but I was talking with Sutton and he believes we will need to sell Wingate estate to have the liquid cash for the hotel expansion."

Ava pulled in a deep breath and nodded. "I figured there would have to be an extreme decision, but the company has to come first."

Luke hated the idea of selling the estate, but Ava was right. The company had to come first. There were so many people depending on them to turn this disaster around, not to mention they had to rebuild their reputation. None of them were quitters and even though selling the estate would be emotional, they would all do what was necessary to start the upward climb.

"I love you both. Thanks for staying by me." Ava smiled and hugged each of her nephews. "I better get back to the party. Great job, by the way. I'm going to see Kelly to tell her what an amazing job she did with the decor."

Once Ava was gone, Luke sipped his bourbon and eyed the full room. He and his brother stood back in the hallway around the corner from the offices. Ava had wanted to talk to them away from the crowd and the noise.

Luke started to shift from leaning against the wall when Zeke stepped to block him.

"One minute."

Luke stared back at his brother. "What?"

"I know I was giving you a hard time about Kelly—"

"We're not doing this again, are we?" Luke asked curtly.

"I just want to make sure you don't hurt her or screw this up," Zeke stated. "The last thing we need is another shake-up on any level at the office. Kelly is the foundation in your department. If things went wrong with you two and she left..."

Luke had already thought of that. He didn't want to lose Kelly in any capacity—personal or professional. He wanted her in all aspects of his life, but that confession would have to wait until they were alone tonight.

And he sure as hell wasn't about to tell his brother how he truly felt for Kelly. That was something she deserved to hear first. He might not be ready to profess his love, but he did want to see where this would go and he fully believed he was falling for her.

"She's not going to leave," Luke stated firmly. "What Kelly and I have going on isn't a big deal or anything for you to worry about. She's been my assistant and she'll always be my assistant."

In the office and in his personal life. He wanted her with him. Damn it, he couldn't wait to get home and tell her.

Home. He liked thinking that she would be home with him. He wondered if she would even be interested in this giant step. After all, they'd only just started seeing each other in an intimate way two weeks ago.

Was this too soon? How the hell would he know if he was making a mistake or not?

Luke didn't know and that risk was both thrilling and terrifying. All he knew for sure was that this was nothing like when he'd been engaged before.

"I'll drop the subject," Zeke told him. "You know I just worry about the company and you and Kelly. She's like a sister to me."

"I get it," Luke said and blew out a sigh. "We better get back out there. I need to make a formal announcement. Care to join me on the stage?"

Zeke nodded. "Sure, but feel free to do the talking."

Luke shook his head and headed down the hall and made his way through the crowd. With his brother at his back, Luke took the three steps to the stage at the end of the ballroom and stepped up to the podium. There were several more easels and large posters propped on the stage showcasing the various resorts from Wingate. Luke was damn proud to be part of this company.

He tapped the mic to make sure it was on and then tapped a little louder to get the attention of the crowd. The roar of the guests started to calm down and Luke cleared his throat.

"First of all, I want to thank you all for coming out tonight to the relaunch of Wingate Enterprises."

A round of applause went up and Luke waited until the noise died down again.

"As you all have seen and heard, we are taking Wingate in a new direction," he announced. "We have a wide variety of packages for romantic getaways and those can be pre-booked starting right now. Every budget was taken into consideration and we have something for everyone."

Luke glanced around the room at all of the familiar faces and couldn't help but smile and be filled with hope at all of the people who had come out to support the company.

"I can't take all of the credit for this brilliant plan," he added. "My assistant Kelly Prentiss has truly been the brains behind the operation. If I could get Kelly to come up here."

He tried to scan the crowd for where she'd be coming from, but he didn't see anyone. Luke glanced to his side where his brother stood, but Zeke just shrugged.

Luke waited another minute, but Kelly never showed. Where could she be? She hadn't mentioned needing to leave.

"Well, I'm sure Kelly is here somewhere," he added with a chuckle. "I know she would appreciate you stopping her and thanking her for putting this amazing party together and helping with this next journey for Wingate Enterprises. Thank you all again for coming and, please, continue to enjoy the open bar and the rest of the evening."

Luke stepped from the podium and off the stage.

"I'm going to look for Kelly," he told his brother. "That's not like her to leave or just be gone. Maybe she's in the back office or the restroom."

Luke checked everywhere and couldn't find her. He pulled his cell from his pocket, but there were no texts or calls from her. He sent her a quick text asking where she was and if everything was okay. He waited a few minutes, but there was no reply.

Now he was starting to worry. As he asked around about anyone seeing her, everyone said they'd just seen her moments ago, so he had to believe she wasn't far.

A loud shout caught his attention, but it was just the Wingate twins laughing and they were being hoisted into the air by some rowdy guests. Clearly people had taken advantage of that open bar.

Luke watched as the rambunctious celebration continued on outside and he saw it coming before it happened. Sutton and Sebastian were launched into the swimming pool by a group of cheering guys.

Was this the equivalent of dumping the ice bucket on the coach at the end of a big win?

Luke had bigger issues to deal with however, and he sure as hell didn't want to be part of that pool club. It might be fairly nice for December, but that didn't mean the pool water was warm.

When he turned back toward the ballroom, he spotted Gracie.

"Hey, Gracie." He stopped in front of her and noted how she looked like she wasn't feeling well. "Have you seen Kelly anywhere?"

"I just spoke to her," Gracie said. "Maybe thirty minutes or an hour ago. Is something wrong?"

He shook his head. "I just can't find her, that's all."

Something caught Gracie's eye over Luke's shoulder and she gasped. Luke turned and saw the Wingate twins dripping by the pool and Sebastian had stripped out of his jacket and shirt. A long scar ran down his back.

When Luke turned back to Gracie, she appeared even paler than before and looked on the verge of passing out.

"Are you alright?" he asked, reaching for her.

"I-I have to go."

She fled the ballroom, and Luke had no idea what had spooked her, but she was gone.

His cell vibrated in his pocket and he pulled it out to see a text from Kelly. Relief spread through him, quickly followed by confusion.

I overheard something you probably didn't intend for me to hear. You need to check your email.

His email? Had something important come through while they'd been at the party and she was working on it now? That would be just like her to take the stress off him and try to get everything taken care of while he was at the party. He smiled as he tapped the email icon. She was too damn good for him.

The confusion grew and along with it came astonishment.

Kelly's resignation letter? The date at the top was today, and she stated the notification was effective immediately. She indicated a difference of goals and her life going in a different direction now.

What the hell?

Luke read it again, still unsure about what was going on. What different direction? Wasn't this the same woman who wanted to talk to him for hours on end when they got home? The same woman who'd worn a dress she thought he would love?

The same damn woman who'd deceived him and

swept him away for a romantic getaway for five days?

Anger slid right on in with all of his other jumbled emotions. Luke sent a text to his brother and Ava that he had to leave and he would get with them later. He assured them nothing was wrong just because he didn't want them to worry, but everything seemed to be wrong right now.

He had no idea where Kelly was or what she was thinking. Her email had been so vague, other than the part where she quit on him without notice or logical reasons.

Luke tried calling her over and over and no answer. She was ignoring him, and he wanted to know why. Whatever she had overheard had made her jump to conclusions and he needed to fix whatever the hell was going on.

He went to his house, hoping to catch her if she went there to retrieve her things. Who knows how long she'd been gone from the party before he realized it?

The moment he pulled into his drive, he saw her car and a heady sense of relief spread through him. At least he knew where she was, now he needed to know what the hell had happened this evening.

He barely had the engine off before he was out of the car and rushing up the stairs to the front door.

He couldn't let her leave without finding out where her head was and who had hurt her.

And then he was going to have to tell her how he truly felt.

Twenty

Kelly heard the front door open and close, and she cursed herself for coming back here to retrieve her things. She should've just gone home and worried about her clothes and toiletries later.

A lump rose in her throat as the events of the night assailed her once again She had been a fool to believe they could have been more. For five years she'd slowly fallen for Luke, calling herself naive every step of the way for allowing thoughts of a relationship with her boss to creep in. She was not only foolish and naive, she was stupid and gullible.

And now she had to move on.

"What are you doing?"

Kelly cringed as she tossed her leggings into the suitcase on the bed. She pulled in a deep breath, willed herself not to cry until she was home alone and turned to face Luke.

"I'm packing," she replied simply. "Did you get my email?"

"Of course I got your email, that's why I'm here." He took a step farther into the room, then another, but he didn't come too close. "What happened at the party to make you want to resign? Did someone say something to you? Why wouldn't you bring the issue to me instead of just disappearing?"

Kelly laughed bitterly. "The issue *is* you," she stressed. "I'm just your assistant, Luke. That's all I'll ever be and what we shared wasn't a big deal, right?"

Her heart started beating even faster when he took another step toward her. "What are you talking about?"

Swallowing her emotions, Kelly crossed her arms over her chest. "I heard you in the hallway talking to your brother. I was coming out of the office from checking on Gracie because she didn't feel well, but I heard you tell him that I was your assistant, that's what I'd always be and he didn't need to worry about what we had going on because it wasn't a big deal."

When he started to take a step forward, she held up her hand. "No," she commanded. "Don't touch me and don't come near me. I shouldn't have let myself get so caught up in my own thoughts and fantasies."

"Kelly—"

"Stop."

She shook her head and went back to the closet to get a few more things. She really wished she would've taken this dress off when she'd gotten back, but she'd been in a hurry to grab her things and leave.

"I just want to get out while I can and save myself any further embarrassment," she went on, grabbing clothes and giving them a toss into the suitcase. "I'm not upset with you, I'm angry at myself. You never promised me anything and you never acted like you wanted more than what we had. I should've made my feelings known so everything was out there between us, but I thought—"

"Kelly," he bellowed to get her attention.

She jerked back and cringed. He was smiling at her. *Smiling.* How dare he smile when she was clearly torn in two and she just wanted to get out of here with some sort of dignity intact.

"What you overheard was just for my brother's sake," he stated. "Zeke kept grilling me on what was going on and I kept telling him it was nothing and you were just my assistant. I didn't want to tell him that I was developing feelings for you, because I wanted to tell you first."

Kelly stilled, her heart in her throat as she tried to process his words. "What?"

Luke slowly closed the gap between them as he continued to hold her gaze and widen that smile.

"I want you to continue staying with me," he told her. "I want more with you, because I'm falling for you."

"Wait…what?"

Luke reached for her and slid his strong hands over her shoulders. "I told Zeke you would always be my assistant because I do always want you by my side. I want to see where this takes us. We're so damn compatible everywhere, did you think I'd honestly want to let you go?"

Kelly pulled in a shaky breath and willed herself not to cry. He wanted her to stay? She was so confused and clearly had almost let miscommunication and eavesdropping ruin her life and her career.

"You're falling for me?" she asked.

"I didn't realize how much so until I saw your email," he admitted. "I knew I wanted you to keep living here and I knew I wanted to try for more… But that ache in my heart and in the pit of my stomach had never been so strong than at the thought of losing you. I'm pretty sure I ran at least one red light to get here."

Kelly closed her eyes and dropped her head between his arms. "I'm so foolish. I just heard that and assumed you were once again putting work ahead of everything else and I couldn't live like that. My mother did and it destroyed her marriage to my dad. I don't want to be miserable like she was."

Luke gently lifted her head and started leaning in.

"You'll never be miserable as long as I'm around," he vowed. "And I'm about to mess up that lipstick you reapplied earlier."

Anticipation quickly replaced sadness and frustration. She tipped her face up to welcome his kiss, and joy flowed through her as his lips hungrily claimed hers. His hands slid down her bare arms and went to her waist as he tugged her closer. Her breasts flattened against his chest and she was so glad he'd come after her. She was so glad he explained what she'd heard. She'd just been so afraid of getting her hopes up that when she overheard him and Zeke talking...

Kelly pushed away those negative thoughts and concentrated on the man who was kissing her, the man who wanted to be with her in his home to see exactly where this relationship could go.

"Did I mention how much I love this dress?" he asked as he eased back.

Kelly nodded. "I believe you mentioned it, but I'm ready to get out of it."

She turned her back to him and glanced over her shoulder. "Care to help me out of this?"

Luke let out a guttural growl as his hands went to the zipper. The dress parted and his warm breath grazed her back, instantly giving her goose bumps.

The garment fell away from her chest and then he was shoving the full skirt on down until it pooled in a thick puddle of material around her ankles.

Luke cursed beneath his breath, and Kelly turned

back around and stepped out of the dress, wearing nothing but her heels and her earrings.

"Have you been like this all night?" he demanded, his voice thick with arousal.

Kelly merely smiled.

"You are trying to kill me."

"I was hoping we'd come back here and you'd strip that off me," she told him. "I figured wasting time with anything beneath was just silly."

He reached for her again, his hands suddenly all over her bare skin.

"I do love how you think," he murmured. "Just make sure you wear the proper clothes to board meetings or I'm not responsible for my actions."

Kelly reached for his suit jacket and slid it off his arms, but before she could get to his buttons, Luke was lifting her in his arms and capturing her lips once again.

He shifted a few steps and her back was against the wall. Then he held her in place with her legs locked around his waist as he fiddled with his pants.

Kelly couldn't help but laugh. "In a hurry?"

His dark eyes locked with hers. "You have no idea."

In the next breath, he joined their bodies and Kelly laced her fingers around his neck and pulled his lips to hers. She wanted all of him right now. She wanted to consume him, she wanted him to feel her love, to know that this was real and she wasn't going anywhere.

He'd come for her. That thought completely overwhelmed her. She'd tried to make an escape and he'd been right after her. The man always went after what he wanted, and now that was *her*.

Kelly had never been so happy or felt so treasured.

Luke reached between them and cupped her breasts as he worked his hips.

"Not fair," she panted.

He nipped at her earlobe. "What?"

"You have too many clothes on."

"Later," he promised. "We'll go slow later."

She liked the sound of that.

Between the ministrations to her chest and the way he worked those talented hips, Kelly was already on the verge. It had been a hell of a night, and she was just too revved up.

She let go and cried out his name as he plastered one hand on the wall next to her head and increased his pace moments before he lost himself in his own climax.

Kelly focused on her breathing, on keeping her shaky legs from falling. She wanted to stay right here, wrapped in Luke's love. She knew he loved her. He'd admitted he was falling for her and all she wanted was to start this new chapter with him.

"Kelly," he murmured against her ear. "Never leave me again. I couldn't stand it."

She smiled and took his face in her hands to ease him back. She wanted to look him in the eye when she told him how she felt.

"I love you, Luke. I'm never going anywhere."

"Good because I need you in every part of my life and I want to be able to tell you every day that I love you, too."

Kelly couldn't suppress her smile or her tears. "This is going to be the best Christmas ever."

He sealed their promise with a kiss and Kelly knew this was only the beginning of their lifelong journey.

* * * * *

#2779 THE RANCHER'S WAGER

Gold Valley Vineyards • by Maisey Yates

No one gets under Jackson Cooper's skin like Cricket Maxfield. When he goes all in at a charity poker match, Jackson loses their bet and becomes her reluctant ranch hand. In close quarters, tempers flare—and the fire between them ignites into a passion that won't be ignored...

#2780 ONE NIGHT IN TEXAS

Texas Cattleman's Club: Rags to Riches • by Charlene Sands

Gracie Diaz once envied the Wingate family—and wanted Sebastian Wingate. Now she's wealthy in her own right—and pregnant with his baby! Was their one night all they'll ever have? Or is there more to Sebastian than she's ever known?

#2781 THE RANCHER

Dynasties: Mesa Falls • by Joanne Rock

Ranch owner Miles Rivera is surprised to see a glamourous woman like Chiara Campagna in Mesa Falls. When he catches the influencer snooping, he's determined to learn what she's hiding. But when suspicion turns to seduction, can they learn to trust one another?

#2782 RUNNING AWAY WITH THE BRIDE

Nights at the Mahal • by Sophia Singh Sasson

Billionaire Ethan Connors crashes his ex's wedding, only to find he's run off with the wrong bride! Divya Singh didn't want to marry and happily leaves with the sexy stranger. But when their fun fling turns serious, can he win over this runaway bride?

#2783 SCANDAL IN THE VIP SUITE

Miami Famous • by Nadine Gonzalez

Looking for the ultimate getaway, writer Nina Taylor is shocked when *her* VIP suite is given to Hollywood bad boy Julian Knight. Their attraction is undeniable, and soon they've agreed to share the room... and the only bed. But will the meddling press ruin everything?

#2784 INTIMATE NEGOTIATIONS

Blackwells of New York • by Nicki Night

Investment banker Zoe Baldwin is determined to make it in the city's thriving financial industry, but when she meets her handsome new boss, Ethan Blackwell, it's hard to keep things professional. As long days turn into hot nights, can their relationship withstand the secrets between them?

YOU CAN FIND MORE INFORMATION ON UPCOMING HARLEQUIN TITLES, FREE EXCERPTS AND MORE AT HARLEQUIN.COM.

HDCNM1220

No one gets under Jackson Cooper's skin like Cricket Maxfield. When he goes all in at a charity poker match, Jackson loses their bet and becomes her reluctant ranch hand. In close quarters, tempers flare—and the fire between them ignites into a passion that won't be ignored...

Read on for a sneak peek at
The Rancher's Wager
by New York Times *bestselling author Maisey Yates!*

Cricket Maxfield had a hell of a hand. And her confidence made that clear. Poor little thing didn't think she needed a poker face if she had a hand that could win.

But he knew better.

She was sitting there with his hat, oversize and over her eyes, on her head and an unlit cigar in her mouth.

A mouth that was disconcertingly red tonight, as she had clearly conceded to allowing her sister Emerson to make her up for the occasion. That bulky, fringed leather jacket should have looked ridiculous, but over that red dress, cut scandalously low, giving a tantalizing wedge of scarlet along with pale, creamy cleavage, she was looking not ridiculous at all.

And right now, she was looking like far too much of a winner.

Lucky for him, around the time he'd escalated the betting, he'd been sure she would win.

He'd wanted her to win.

"I guess that makes you my ranch hand," she said. "Don't worry. I'm a very good boss."

Now, Jackson did not want a boss. Not at his job, and not in his bedroom. But her words sent a streak of fire through his blood. Not because he wanted her in charge. But because he wanted to show her what a boss looked like.

Cricket was...

A nuisance. If anything.

That he had any awareness of her at all was problematic enough. Much less that he had any awareness of her as a woman. But that was just because of what she was wearing. The truth of the matter was, Cricket would turn back into the little pumpkin she usually was once this evening was over and he could forget all about the fact that he had ever been tempted to look down her dress during a game of cards.

"Oh, I'm sure you are, sugar."

"I'm your boss. Not your sugar."

"I wasn't aware that you winning me in a game of cards gave you the right to tell me how to talk."

"If I'm your boss, then I definitely have the right to tell you how to talk."

"Seems like a gray area to me." He waited for a moment, let the word roll around on his tongue, savoring it so he could really, really give himself all the anticipation he was due. "Sugar."

"We're going to have to work on your attitude. You're insubordinate."

"Again," he said, offering her a smile, "I don't recall promising a specific attitude."

There was activity going on around him. The small crowd watching the game was cheering, enjoying the way this rivalry was playing out in front of them. He couldn't blame them. If the situation wasn't at his expense, then he would have probably been smirking and enjoying himself along with the rest of the audience, watching the idiot who had lost to the little girl with the cigar.

He might have lost the hand, but he had a feeling he'd win the game.

Don't miss what happens next in...
The Rancher's Wager
by New York Times *bestselling author Maisey Yates!*

Available January 2021 wherever
Harlequin Desire books and ebooks are sold.

Harlequin.com

**IF YOU ENJOYED THIS BOOK
WE THINK YOU WILL ALSO LOVE**

HARLEQUIN

PRESENTS

Escape to exotic locations where passion knows no bounds.

Welcome to the glamorous lives of royals and billionaires, where passion knows no bounds. Be swept into a world of luxury, wealth and exotic locations.

8 NEW BOOKS AVAILABLE EVERY MONTH!